about the editor

PETER WILD is the coauthor of *Before the Rain* and the editor of *Perverted by Language: Fiction Inspired by the Fall* and *The Flash*. His fiction has appeared in numerous journals, e-zines, anthologies, and magazines, including *Dogmatika, 3:AM Magazine, NOÖ Journal, SNReview, Word Riot, Straight from the Fridge, Thieves Jargon, Pindeldyboz, Pen Pusher, Scarecrow, The Beat, Litro,* and *Dreams That Money Can Buy*. He lives in Manchester with his wife and three children.

noise
fiction inspired by sonic youth

edited by peter wild

introduction by lee ranaldo

HARPER ● PERENNIAL

NEW YORK ● LONDON ● TORONTO ● SYDNEY ● NEW DELHI ● AUCKLAND

HARPER PERENNIAL

Originally published in the United Kingdom in 2008 by Serpent's Tail, an imprint of Profile Books Ltd.

HarperCollins books may be purchased for educational, business, or sales promotional use. For information please write: Special Markets Department, HarperCollins Publishers, 10 East 53rd Street, New York, NY 10022.

FIRST U.S. EDITION

Designed and typeset at Neuadd Bwll, Llanwrtyd Wells

Library of Congress Cataloging-in-Publication Data is available upon request.

ISBN 978-0-06-166929-3

09   10   11   12   13   RRD   10   9   8   7   6   5   4   3   2   1

For Andrew Wild

contents

cornfield webs:
an introduction

lee ranaldo

||||||||||||||||||||||||||||||

You can get a lot of information out of a song title. A good title says it all, sometimes. Many writers – song or otherwise – begin with a title, some nugget that provides a stimulating point from which to leap off into a void, some road sign that points a way forward. Find the groovy, the hip, the mysterious or enlightening turn of phrase, then grab it and press onwards from there. You might say that the twenty some-odd years of Sonic Youth song titles, taken as a whole, tell a vision of sorts, adding up to their own little cosmology after all these years. A universe willed into existence. Enter thru song title after song title to new windows on the world...

Inside we'll find twenty-one new visions based on Sonic Youth titles, re-purposed to new ends. Aside from whatever empathy the twenty-one authors in this collection have for our music, we can at the very least observe that they have found within our catalogue some titles for inspiration. Do these writings reflect back on the

noise

band itself? Is there some clandestine history of Sonic Youth to be decoded from these pages? A secret map into the heart of the band?

Dots may be connected in many alternating patterns, this way and that, as each eye sees it, until we end up with something that looks like the webs of those spiders in LSD experiments: complicated and chaotic, barely knowable. Unintelligible? Perhaps, but also possibly like music is, sometimes: unable to put easily into words. Midnight on the moon... The diamond sea... Thought-waves on a beach dissolving...

Twenty-one authors are presented here with Sonic Youth as some sort of unifying theory. Are they responding to the music itself? The work ethic? Some epiphany they had at a gig out in a cornfield somewhere, as we played on in the furious distorted bliss of rapturous feedback? Are they pushing against the 'legend'? Over-familiarity with the brand breeding a sort of contempt? Could it be some inspiration derived from the network of contributors and collaborators that we've presented/befriended/championed/raved about? For in a rather large sense our time as a band has been defined by the community we've fostered, a sense of inclusion that we've hoped to convey.

It doesn't ultimately matter how directly (or not) these twenty-one stories reference Sonic Youth. Somehow the spirit of the band has been inspiring enough to these scribes that they've agreed to participate in this project. Empty pages? Or full of... what?!? Let's turn a leaf and see what they've come up with...

death to our friends

—j robert lennon

What I like about Sonic Youth is that they like to rip it apart and put it back together again. Their instruments, their songs, everything. This is a good way to treat the raw materials of art.

Here is how I found out what I was.

I lived in a dormitory, a college dormitory, in a tiny room with one bed. I shared the room with a room-mate, a girl I hated, because she was mean and made me sleep on the floor and never once looked me in the eye. And every morning I would pretend to be asleep while she stomped around the room, and once she was gone I would get up and put on my clothes and leave for class through the same door, which led out on to the grassy quad. I was so happy, those mornings, to emerge into light and air and freedom – I didn't like living in the dorm, I was so lonely, and it seemed to me like I'd been sleeping there on the floor for ever.

There was a little girl I used to see, in the stairwell. She was black haired, round faced, and always wore a white dress. Maybe she was eight. She sat on the radiator and watched me hurry past on my way to class. I wondered about her sometimes – whose child she was, why she loitered there in the stairwell – but never spoke to her. I suppose I should have. But I was eighteen, and children didn't interest me, and the girl did not seem friendly. I only wanted to leave the dormitory. I wanted the light and air. I didn't want to stop and talk to a chubby little girl.

Then one day I did stop. She was there, on the radiator as always, and I came running down the stairs with my book sack over my shoulder, and she hopped down and on to the landing and stood before me, blocking my way.

I stopped. I stopped and looked into her eyes, and saw surprise there, and triumph.

'You stopped,' the girl said to me.

'You're in my way!'

'Other people don't stop for me.'

'They would,' I said, 'if you stood in front of them like that. Now excuse me,' I went on, 'I have to get to class.'

But the little girl didn't move. 'What class are you going to?' she asked me.

'That's none of your business,' I said.

'But I want to know.'

'I bet you do.'

'Tell me.'

Well. There she was, standing in my way. And I was in a hurry. And so I figured I might as well just tell her the answer to her question. But I couldn't seem to bring it to mind. That is, I knew, of course – I was in a great hurry, and people who don't know where they're going are rarely in a hurry to get there – but for some reason I couldn't remember at that particular moment.

I must have hesitated, because she said, 'Why don't you look in your bag?'

And I said, 'No.'

'Why not?'

Again, I didn't have a good answer. She took a step forward, slid my book sack off my shoulder, and opened it up. I suppose I knew then. I just stood there and watched her.

Stones. Little stones and dead leaves. And other bits of trash, bits of paper, plastic soda-can rings, bottle tops, a toilet paper roll. All dried and dusted. That's what was in my book sack.

'You're like me,' the girl said. 'I knew it. I knew you were!'

'I'm not anything like you,' I said, knowing now, knowing I was wrong. Really, I had known all along. I was just pretending. I looked down at my dress, my filthy torn dry dress, cotton shirtwaist with a convertible collar and roll-up sleeves, and buttons down below the waist. I remembered buying it, with my mother. I was so happy and excited to be going to college! It was 1964. I was eighteen.

I was still eighteen. I would always be eighteen. I would always live in the dorm. I sat down on the steps and the little girl sat next to me and took my hand in hers, and when students came thundering down the stairs they didn't stop, they didn't say excuse me or tell us to move, they just barrelled right through, they went right through us and out the door to their classes.

That was fifteen years ago, I think. It's hard to keep track. The girl's name is Annabel. She is the daughter, the only child, of a professor of history who once lived here as a faculty adviser. Annabel died falling down the stairs – she died on the landing, when the building was still new.

As for me, I killed myself, I'm afraid. I jumped off the Zabriskie Bridge and into Reston Gorge. You'll think that was foolish but perhaps it wasn't. There was something in me that had wanted it my whole life. Most girls, leaving home for school, fantasise about smoking, or drinking, or making love to boys in the privacy of their own rooms. I don't mean to be dramatic, but I think what I anticipated most eagerly was the freedom to die. I had been hospitalised several times when I was in high school, briefly, and once I slit my wrists in the bath. But I had convinced my parents I was past all that. I may even have convinced myself. And then I came here, and the weather was so cold, and I walked over that gorge every morning, and it was so deep, so real. There was a boy, too, of course, something has to set these things off – he said he loved me, then he left me – and at the time that's what I was certain had made me do it. But no, it was me. I wanted it. I had longed for it.

Why did it take me so long to admit to myself what I had done? It was the sense of relief – my body was gone, and with it the despair it had harboured. My head no longer ached, my hands didn't tremble when I met a stranger. My heavy heart no longer made me fall asleep during the day or keep me awake at night. How wonderful life would have been, had it been like this! I lived with whomever wouldn't notice me, which was most people. A few sensed there was something wrong. A few could feel me passing in the hall, saw a flash of motion out of the corner of their eye. One girl could smell the water on me. One heard my bare feet slide along the floor. Those

I left alone. The oblivious I stayed close to. I did what they did. I lived their lives as if they were my own.

But once Annabel showed me the truth, I became her friend. She wasn't a normal eight-year-old girl. She had watched almost seventy years of life go by. She was wise. She introduced me to the others. Some of them were mean, and looked away when I extended my hand to them; others were all right. Either way, no one wanted to be friends, no one but Annabel. There was something wrong with being this way – remaining in the world – and nobody liked to be reminded they were doing it. Socialising must have seemed somehow sick to them. They snubbed us.

But I bucked the trend. I always was different. I didn't mind being what I was, didn't think there was anything strange about it. People are just as stuck up in death as they are in life – at least they are here. Never facing up to uncomfortable truths, always looking down on others. Anyway, Annabel and I were lonely. The fact was, we weren't compatible – we wouldn't have been friends in life. She was too reserved, too serious. But we agreed that we were lonely, and so we started helping things along.

We look for the sad ones, the sad ones who are sweet, and we give them a little push. When they walk over the bridge, *my* bridge, I gently take their face in my hands and turn it, ever so gently, towards the water. When one of them puts a knife away, Annabel moves it back where it belongs, out in the open, to be seen and contemplated. The sleeping pills, the antidepressants that they safely stow away in the cabinet – we take them out. We leave them open, on the edge of the sink.

We don't kill them. We're not capable of that, and wouldn't even if we were. We just find the ones for whom the only impediment to death is fear. And we give them a nudge. Just a little one.

So far we've failed. Some of them reject us, they move away, or change their minds about life. The ones we've shepherded into death, most of those slip by us – we get a glimpse of them, coming up out of the gorge or getting up from the bed, and maybe we catch their eye, but they can't be convinced to stop, or maybe they're powerless to try. They rise, fade, expand, vanish. They go somewhere else. Maybe someplace better. Maybe not.

And then there are the ones who stay in this world. Most of those are like the others. They reject us. Perhaps they're confused, or disappointed. Some will turn nasty, and some may remain indifferent. And like the others, they may eventually drift off and disappear. Regardless, there is nothing quite like the expression on their faces as the physical world gives way, and they emerge into lightness. The terror, the pain, lingers for the faintest moment, like an echo, and then they're gone. The skin smooths, the scars fade. Everything becomes simple.

Someday we'll find our friend. We talk about this person all the time. Annabel thinks it will be a woman – it was hard for her, watching her mother grieve, losing her to the world, and she has never gotten over that loss. But I believe – I hope – our friend will be a man. He could be a lover to me, after a fashion; and to Annabel he could be both son and father, for she is both an old woman and a little girl. I imagine this man, young and beautiful, miserable and kind – I imagine him standing up from his cold bones and taking my hands, with relief and gratitude. I imagine us walking hand in hand – our friend in the middle, with Annabel and me on either side – out across the quad, and away from this campus, to whatever it is that lies beyond it. What that might be, I've forgotten. The physical world no longer seems quite real to me any more, beyond what I see every day.

But this imaginary man, he is real. Perhaps he hasn't yet been born, but he is real. He will grow up to meet his fate here, and Annabel and I will be waiting for him, when he emerges stunned and battered out of death, and into the arms of friends.

disappearer

matt thorne

Some writers can't write without silence; others without listening to music. I fall in the latter category. Sonic Youth's music is so good to write to because the lyrics always seem to be pointing to something secret that's not explicitly expressed. I chose 'Disappearer' as the inspiration for my story because there's something deliberately missing at the centre of the song (is it a star, man, woman or car that's gone?), just as there's something deliberately missing from my story.

Michael Chambers liked empty restaurants. He was a solitary person who'd grown up with an overprotective mother and no dad and as a child he'd had emotional problems. His mother had paid for him to see a counsellor who told him that while it wasn't a good idea to isolate himself, there was no shame in going to a gig or film or party on his own. He'd taken this to heart: in his teenage years it had given him a mystique that had ironically led to more people being interested in him than if he'd tried to get popular in a conventional way, but now he was in his mid-thirties it meant he was mostly alone. He had a nocturnal job, where he worked solo, seven days a week, transferring old videos on to DVD for a rich eighties comedian who kept his identity secret. There was another guy who did the same job during the day but they only saw each other for five minutes at midnight and noon. Sleeping all day made it hard for Michael to make arrangements to see friends and, as he lived alone in London, very few people bothered to keep in contact. He liked to make the most of the five hours he had each day and an important part of this was choosing where to eat. Almost every gig he went to now was in an isolated area – he didn't understand why American noise-acts had colonised carpet shops in Dalston or lock-ups round the back of the Elephant and Castle tube station – but at least it gave him plenty of restaurants in the surrounding area to choose from. Tonight he'd found a Vietnamese restaurant that clearly suffered from being just too far from the popular strip of similar establishments and at 7.30 on a Monday evening was completely empty.

This excited Michael. An empty restaurant wasn't as novel as an empty cinema – no matter how poorly reviewed or obscure a film there were always at least a couple of other audience members at every screening he attended – but it was a desirable prospect nonetheless. Because he had to spend all night every night in front of a screen, Michael tried not to watch television at home, but on the rare occasions he did there always seemed to be teaser ads for programmes about restaurants. He'd always believed celebrity chefs had an easy ride – if you were any good your talent would soon be recognised. He knew that some believed the same was true of music or literature, but Michael didn't agree. There were plenty of bands and authors he admired who failed to find much of an audience. He liked to believe that the cooks in empty restaurants were like obscure bands or authors, giving their best irrespective of whether they'd ever achieve the acclaim they deserved. Of course, cooks were performing under firmer restrictions, but he wanted to believe that a lonely man in the kitchen of an empty restaurant cared as much about the consistency of his sweet-and-sour sauce as Peter Gordon did about his signature dish.

He entered tonight's restaurant. He didn't yet know what kind of unpopular restaurant this would be. Some unpopular restaurants had unpleasant waiters and it was hard to tell whether they were angry because no one came there or whether no one came there because the waiters were angry. Other unpopular restaurants employed waiters who fell upon any customers in an off-putting way, ensuring anyone who entered would be so embarrassed they'd never return. As Michael rarely went back to the same restaurant he didn't mind whether the waiters were rude or over-attentive and found it bore no relation to the quality of the food.

Tonight's waitress was of the over-attentive breed, and she even committed the shocking intimacy of placing her hand on the small of Michael's back as she guided him to his table. He was surprised by this, but didn't say anything. Instead of giving him a chance to look over the menu, she hovered beside him, waiting for his order. Michael wasn't a gourmet, but he often chose the most expensive dish on the menu for the sheer hell of it – and as the anonymous comedian paid him well for working antisocial hours and he had few expenses, he could easily afford it. Lobster was his favourite food, but he often found in these sorts of restaurants that you had to order it a day in advance. As this didn't seem to be the case here, he asked for it.

The waitress winced. 'I'm really sorry, sir, we don't do lobster any more. It should've been taken off the menu.'

'That's OK,' he said, 'I'll have…'

'Perhaps you would like the crab,' she suggested.

Michael considered this. He rarely ate crab, considering it poor man's lobster rather than a dish in its own right. But now that the waitress had suggested it he found himself feeling an overwhelming desire to fill his mouth with the meat of this inferior crustacean, and he told the waitress that he would indeed like the crab. She smiled and, seemingly emboldened by his acceptance of her suggestion, asked him whether he would like a beer with his food.

He didn't often drink alcohol with his dinner when he was out alone. Sometimes it was ages before the band came onstage at these smaller clubs and, if he had too many drinks beforehand, he got tired and bored and even the surge of excitement he always felt when a band walked out onstage and picked up their instruments wasn't enough to perk him up and he'd leave after a couple of songs. But there were four bands on the bill tonight, which meant there wouldn't be too much waiting around, and he wasn't likely to stay until the end anyway, so he told the waitress he would like a beer.

'Tiger, Asahi or Tsing Tao?'

Her pen hovered above her pad as she waited for Michael's reply. When he did drink beer in these sorts of restaurants and it was on the menu, he'd usually have a Tiger, but he thought that as he was having crab instead of lobster, he should have a beer he normally wouldn't drink as well.

'Tsing Tao, please.'

The waitress nodded and asked him whether he wanted plain or egg-fried rice. Then she returned to the kitchen. Michael never brought anything with him to read when he went to restaurants alone. He enjoyed the experience of waiting for food. Lacking experiences in his daily life when he was engaged in normal social interactions, the five or ten or fifteen minutes he spent most days between ordering his dinner and waiting for it to arrive was an important time for him. The waitress came back with his Tsing Tao and the metal cracker and thin forks he would need to eat his crab.

He picked up the cracker, examining the design. The handles were in the shape of lobster claws. The waitress noticed him doing this and smiled at him. He had the strange sense she was flirting. He rarely received attention from women and, when he did, they failed to stay around for long, unable to understand what they saw as his fatal lack of ambition. The possibility that this elegantly dressed Vietnamese woman – who, he was beginning to suspect, wasn't just a waitress, but was the owner of the restaurant – would be interested in a disaffected thirty-something in a Viking Moses T-shirt was hard for him to believe, but when she returned with his crab and the egg-fried rice, she leaned over him and carefully demonstrated the best way to use the cracker in a way that made him feel uncomfortably aroused.

He had never been in a situation like this before. The closest he'd come to having sex with a stranger was picking up a woman he didn't know at a party thrown by a college friend. He wasn't psychologically equipped to deal with what he saw as the woman's advances and as she kept returning to his table to fill his beer glass or ask whether he was enjoying the crab he tried to imagine what might happen if he did kiss her. He wondered whether it was the emptiness of the restaurant that was exciting her; her knowledge that if he did make a move she could turn the sign over from open to closed and no one would disturb them.

He ate his food quickly and, although she tried to entice him into having another beer or dessert, he ignored her and asked for the bill. He checked his wallet, wanting to pay with cash so he could speed up his exit, but he'd forgotten to get any money from the hole-in-the-wall. He took out his debit card and put it inside the black leather folder she'd placed in front of him.

Instead of taking the folder away, she opened it and squinted at the name on his card.

'I don't believe it,' she said.

'What?' he asked, worried.

'Your name is Michael Chambers?'

'Yes.'

'We have Michael Chambers upstairs.'

'What?'

'Another Michael Chambers.'

'I don't understand.'

'I own this whole building. Downstairs, as you can see, there is this restaurant. Upstairs there are three flats.'

'OK.'

'And in one of these flats, I have a tenant and his name is Michael Chambers.'

'Ah,' said Michael, relieved.

'You must meet him,' she said, grabbing his hand.

'No,' he replied, pulling his hand away. 'I'm sorry, I'm late for a concert.'

She looked puzzled. 'But you must meet him. How often does something like this happen?' She considered for a moment. 'If you come upstairs and meet him, your meal will be on the house.'

Michael didn't care about money: he had more than enough for his purposes. The prospect of meeting his doppelgänger frightened him, but the woman was so insistent he worried there was no way of escaping the restaurant without doing so. He tried one last protest. 'I'll come back another night.'

'No,' she said, 'it has to be tonight.'

He sighed and got up from the table. She led him to a doorway at the back of the restaurant. They pushed through the string curtain door-divider that separated the kitchen from the restaurant. He almost tripped over a white box of Asahi beer. A Vietnamese man in a white apron smiled at Michael from the other side of a plastic-topped table where he was carefully picking noodles from an orange colander. Michael didn't like seeing the kitchen and, although there was no sign that the preparation of food here was anything but hygienic, he knew he could never come to this restaurant again.

The waitress unlocked a door in the corner of the kitchen that led to a flight of stairs. It occurred to Michael that maybe this whole doppelgänger thing was just a ruse to get him upstairs to an empty bedroom so she could make love to him, and he thought that, although this was an extremely weird seduction technique, if it did turn out to be the case, he wouldn't be angry. Maybe she'd done it before: that could be why the cook had smiled at him.

They went up the stairs and on to the landing. As they approached the door to the other Michael Chambers' bedroom, Michael thought he could hear scratching sounds coming from within. He turned to the waitress.

'Is he OK in there?' he asked.

'What?' she said.

'Those noises...'

'I can't hear anything.'

The noises grew louder. Michael turned round. The waitress was behind him, blocking the landing. She shrugged. 'He drinks a lot, that's all. But he'll be very pleased to see you.'

She crowded right up behind Michael and unlocked the door. As it swung open, he felt her hand on the small of his back again. She gave him a sudden shove and, as he passed over the room's threshold, Michael Chambers ceased to exist.

that's all i know (right now)

katherine dunn

Sonic Youth often operates in that foggy zone between real and surreal, the fact and the fear that may be a wish. I chose this title because it has a proper humility about knowing the difference.

||||||||||||||||||||||||||||||||||

It's been a month now since the severed human hand was found in the public park on my street. There may be city parks where a mere disembodied hand, loose on the grass, would have little impact. But this park has noble old trees, lush lawns around elegant flower beds, benches, paved paths and a children's play area. It is a shared pride for the apartment dwellers in this tony and peaceful old neighbourhood. Litter is rare and frowned upon. In fine weather, sunbathers and band concerts crowd the grass. Children and chess players and sedate dog-walkers commune there from dawn to dusk all year long.

After dark, it's true, other uses and other users occupy the park.

But usually they are gone by daybreak when the park takes on its graceful form. To the taxpaying residents, the hand appearing in this place was a brutal invasion from a world belonging to headlines about the poor sections across the river.

I learned about the hand the day after its discovery from the woman who is captain of the Neighbourhood Crime Patrol. Her two large, limping dogs are always with her when she stomps around the streets at night in her orange vest with her police-issue cell phone, and a big flashlight. But on this sunny autumn afternoon the dogs were stretched snoozing on the sidewalk, the bees were crooning their death songs in the shrubbery and the vivacious Crime Patrol captain was telling the tale to another neighbour when I happened by.

The captain sees the hand as evidence of the satanic covens conducting abuse rituals in two apartment buildings on my street. I know both addresses well and it's clear that she has misinterpreted appearances so I didn't respond to her story until I could talk to John, who lives just around the corner, and who reportedly found the hand.

He's a kind man but nervous and he works in public relations. He is horrified by any kind of unpleasantness. He shares his immaculate apartment with a small dog named Daisy.

I saw him passing my building that same afternoon and rushed out to the sidewalk to demand his version. He was reluctant and would have hurried away but I crouched down to scratch Daisy's chest. John would never be so rude as to yank his dog away from the attention she craves, so he was forced to answer my questions. He winced but confirmed the story.

He and Daisy were out for their pre-breakfast stroll through the park when he came upon three fellow dog-walkers, milling near the abstract metal sculpture on the east lawn. (In the captain's version it was near the public restroom at the opposite end of the park.) They were holding their excited dogs on tight leashes. Thinking there was a bird or some other wild animal on the grass, John kept Daisy near his knee and peered over someone's shoulder.

There on the grass was a human hand severed by a straight, clean cut just above the wrist. There was a trail of 'very bloody blood', as he called it, leading away on the concrete walk.

Surely, I interrupted, it was a rubber hand from a novelty shop – a joke hand with the bone and shreds of torn muscle painted on. John's face lifted for a moment as he considered the possibility, but then sank back into anxious gloom. No. He was familiar with the rubber hands. He'd seen mine hanging on my front door every Halloween. But no. This was different. And one of the other dog-walkers had touched it and turned it over as he watched.

John thought it was probably a man's hand but he couldn't be certain. It was fairly large and bloated, with an unhealthy bluish tinge that made him think of gangrene. But he didn't touch it or sniff it. He didn't let Daisy nose it. He simply looked. One of the others used a cell phone to call the police. They stood waiting for a patrol car. John felt ill and went home.

John is a delightful neighbour, usually cheerful and always gracious. But he is a singularly unsatisfactory witness. He knew the names of the dogs at the scene – Ralph, a schnauzer, Jiggs, an ageing brindle boxer, and Toko, a mop-haired mutt wearing a harness. But he didn't know their owners.

If I had seen the hand I would have registered the condition of its fingernails – dirty? chewed? manicured? painted or polished? – and whether there were visible hairs on the fingers and back, whether any calluses, tattoos, scars or wounds were visible. Certainly I would have checked for the reek of chemical preservatives or other telltale scents. I would have a clear sense of whether the hand was male or female, fresh or rotting, raw or preserved.

And that trail of blood. Was it thick enough to represent a living arm still pumping towards its lost extremity? Or was it just drips, such as might fall in the process of carrying an already long-amputated paw to this place in the grass? And what colour was this 'bloody blood'? Bright or dark would suggest how long the hand had lain there.

But I didn't ask John these questions. Pressing him to dwell on details would have been cruel and useless. He didn't notice such things. As it was, he gave me an injured look and said he'd nearly forgotten the whole thing until I'd brought it up. He hurried away, pulling Daisy after him.

I am still looking for the other witnesses. I ask every dog-walker with an appropriate breed the name of their pooch. Surely one of those three at the scene would have noticed more than John did. But there are many dogs in the neighbourhood and I have yet to find Ralph, Jiggs or Toko.

The crime watch captain was furious at her usual allies, the police. They would not discuss the affair beyond confirming that a hand was, in fact, found in the stated place at the given time. They offered no information about their investigation or their suspicions. No mention of the hand has yet appeared in the news.

This lack of information naturally fuelled a festival of speculation. There was, for the moment, neither war nor election, scandal nor disaster, to engage us. The mystery of the hand was refreshingly small and localised. The captain spread the word. The grocery checkers, pharmacy clerks and coffee servers collected comments from customers and passed them on. Every clot of two or three strollers stalled on the sidewalk was gossiping about the hand. The park benches were prime venues where the debaters could jump up and demonstrate elements of their imagined scenario at the very scene of the crime. The outdoor cafés on the avenue were swept by talk of the hand. The topic gradually enveloped table after table, evicting the usual discussions of politics and business, parking problems and looming divorces through warm afternoons and evenings.

While some clung to an injured or indignant air, many of us passed quickly to enjoyment and a surprising energy. It was a sudden fad, a kind of parlour game, to advance theories regarding the hand's source and saga. Each theory attracted its own fans and boosters. My own thinking took two routes involving either murder or the medical school.

Considering the innocuous option first:

The medical school on the hill is several miles away, but this is a mobile culture of cars and drivers. Our neighbourhood apartment buildings, so close to the hospital and the nursing school, are desirable locations for medical students, interns and nurses. Say, for example, that the anatomy class party goes late. A scalpel-wielding prankster takes off with a memento from the study corpse. Discards it drunkenly. This sequence strikes me as petty but possible.

And then there is murder. The vulgar crime rate is low in this part of town. We are not some trailer park by the racetrack, swamped by used-car lots and deep-fry joints. Not for us the midnight stick-up of convenience stores, the hysterical clubbing of robbery victims or the drive-by shootings and barroom stabbing of crasser neighbourhoods. Our few treasured murders are crimes of passion. And the most common murder victims in the neighbourhood are our brilliant and beautiful gay men. Some are adventurers bringing volatile found objects home from the clubs. In other cases, some true lovers' quarrel escalates to fatal heat. Usually the victims are found in their apartments. If they live alone, it may take time for the tenants next door to complain about a smell.

But a room-mate murderer might try to hide the crime and keep the apartment. The perpetrator could dismember the body in the tub. Lug the pieces out in black plastic garbage bags late at night. The park has big ornamental garbage bins, emptied daily into the city's trucks. Or say the park is a discreet short cut to where our murderer's car is parked. He means to sling the bag into the trunk and drive down to the river. But a plastic bag could rip – a hand could fall out. At night, in the dark beneath the trees, it would be easy to overlook one chunk, to drag the torn bag away, leaving a blood trail, not noticing what had been left behind.

Granted, murder is far from common here, even with tens of thousands of us packed into this well-upholstered section of the city. Still, it has been a good four years since the last and I figure we are due.

For reasons that are not clear to me, these perfectly simple and reasonable possibilities were impatiently dismissed by my neighbours. This snub occurred several days after the discovery when I offered my ideas to those assembled at the five outdoor tables at the corner café. Their immediate and unanimous view was that my scenarios were more sensational than likely. Worse, they were viewed as trite. There were ill-disguised hints to the effect that such notions were somehow typical of me and less than likeable.

Uneasy at having my ideas so abruptly and rudely discounted, I subsided to listen as others presented their theories. Apparently the game had developed rules that I was not aware of. It was soon obvious that the theorists' temperament and politics affected their choice of explanatory tales. But on one factor the radicals and moderates, the timid, the imaginative and the bony-nosed pragmatics seemed to agree. They all presumed that the hand was severed in some blameless fashion, and that the rest of the body was either still alive or previously and innocently dead.

Most of their notions revolved around some combination of three significant elements in the neighbourhood. First, the huge and sprawling Good Samaritan Hospital is just six blocks north of the park. Next, the small but potent Hennessey, Gooch & McGee funeral parlour is even closer to the park, a mere three blocks to the south-east. And finally, our neighbourhood, although renovated to an expensive polish, has become a haven for a homeless spectrum of wino panhandlers and shopping-cart people driven out of the nearby river district by police purges.

In one set of theories, the hand came from the hospital. It was amputated to save a diabetic or an accident victim. Or: it was the useless refuse of an industrial accident, a mill worker who fell into the saw (these explanations acknowledge John's description of the cut as being straight and clean). Say the foreman tossed the hand into an ice bucket and slid it into the ambulance beside the victim, but by the time he arrived at the hospital it was useless. It couldn't be reattached. Or he was dead.

Whatever its origin, surgical or accidental, it was dropped into a waste basin in the hospital operating room, transported to a disposal bag, then tossed by mistake into a dumpster rather than into the big incinerator which disposes of medical waste materials. In times past, we have collected or concocted horror stories about that incinerator and the narrow red-brick chimney that towers over the hospital. It spews the faint high smoke, we suppose, of aborted fetuses, cast-off spleens and tumours, bags of bloody bandages and the endless toxic detritus of illness.

So, the hospital theorists say, this hand lands in a dumpster by mistake and one of the local dumpster-browsers finds it wrapped in plastic and carries it off. These thinkers apparently ran dry before fully developing the dumpster-to-park process.

Anywhere else in town we might speculate that a prowling dog could have accomplished the same thing, snatching the hand out of hospital trash, carrying it to the park. But, in this quarter, the dogs do not prowl. They are as well bred, pampered and meticulously groomed as the local children. Actually dogs far outnumber children among the young and ambitious who live here. Dogs are always leashed. Roaming free is not an option. Even the homeless keep their mongrels tied close because a loose dog would quickly be hauled off to the pound and the vulnerable owner jailed or at least fined.

Besides, a dog would gnaw, would chew. Unless it were one of the soft-mouthed retrievers, a Labrador or golden, and they are not as popular now as in times past. They have been replaced by terriers suitable to apartments and by heavy Rottweilers and wolfhounds, which have supplanted the old-fashioned Dobermans and shepherds as bodyguards. Besides, John, the meek master of the dainty terrier Daisy, would surely have noticed any obvious bite marks or chewed areas on the hand.

A rival but similar scenario traced the hand back to the pristine courtyard of the funeral parlour. Say, for example, a corpse arrives in pieces – a traffic victim whose separated bits are tossed into the body bag at the scene and delivered on a gurney.

One sophisticated version combined the hospital with the funeral premises and the street denizens. A man whose hand is being amputated dies on the operating table and the hand is included for symmetry's sake when the remains are carted off to the mortuary. Careless morticians transfer the body to the work table or cold storage, but the hand remains in the zipper bag, and the bag lies by the loading door to be sanitised later.

Then a prying wanderer – one of our panhandlers, for example – peeks in a door left open for the last summer air, and finds the prize, carries it off, swinging it merrily by one finger… The intent would be entertainment. A prop for ghost tales. A memento for gloomy pondering over a jug of Mad Night beneath the bough. Or a gleeful prank to slip into some crony's ragged blanket, to prop by his face as a surprise for when he wakes. And when he does wake he hurls the thing away on to the grass and chases after the joker, furious, to thrash him. Exeunt clowns down dawn streets, gibbering.

We do not know which hand it was, right or left, because we are all afraid to ask John, who considers us ghouls.

But suppose, said someone else, that it was an accident victim found in the mountains days after a fatal fall, or perhaps it was a drowning. The body decaying out of doors or in the river would account for the bloated flesh. Then suppose this was the left hand and there was jewellery – not a watch because that could be unbuckled or slipped off easily, but say a bracelet, a heavy gold chain too tight to slip off over the swollen, disfigured extremity. The swelling may have extended up the arm, burying the bracelet in the wrist.

Perhaps some sub-mortuarian has been humiliated by the funeral director. Say this brooding tech spies the gold and uses a handy funerary tool to sever the bulky hand and slip the bracelet off the wrist... but then why would she take the hand away with her? To disguise the loss. No, ma'am, she might say, that hand must have been lost in the wreck, he arrived handless, as you see him, and if any bracelet were attached it must be lying in the brush of the gorge, or the bottom of the river. Terrible, terrible...

One of the proponents of this theft theory declared that it was equally applicable to the shadier levels of the hospital staff. The actual doctors and many of the nurses and technicians live in the neighbourhood. They are slim, like the other residents. They drink high-octane coffee in flavours at the outdoor cafés. They shop for aubergine and endive, pilaf and focaccia beside us at the grocery. But this affair of the hand triggered a resurrection of vile, old aspersions about the habits and hygiene of the wider people in green work pyjamas who arrive and leave the hospital on buses. They are seen to buy microwaved lunches at the convenience store across the street from the employee entrance. They are thought to empty bedpans, change filthy sheets, scrub tainted surfaces and pump the gas jets beneath the chimney.

These green-clad wage invaders from across the river have incited our suspicions before – most notably during the last labour contract dispute when their striking pickets were wrongly associated with several late-night bricks through the plate glass of boutiques on the avenue. An ill-timed spate of ferocious rhetoric ended when the brick hurlers were found to be a larking trio of our own cosseted adolescents.

Some at the café tables that night recalled this old embarrassment and objected to targeting the hospital workers. Accusations of blatant classism erupted, and the resulting scornful exchanges threatened to halt the game entirely with a series of flouncing or stomping exits.

The freelance web designer rescued us from our bitterness by flippantly hypothesising that a bird flew over and dropped the hand. Others seized on this immediately, proposing that it could have been one of the many gulls thriving this close to the river. The voracious and indiscriminant gull has both the appetite and the size to carry a substantial hand.

An Audubon member reminded us of the pair of turkey buzzards frequenting the crest of the hill behind us. If a gull or a buzzard were involved, the relieved theorists proposed, the hand might have come from anywhere – a collapsed cemetery in the hills, oozing open in the heavy fall rains. Despite the presence of Hennessey, Gooch & McGee's esteemed funeral parlour, there is no cemetery within miles of our neighbourhood.

The bird image captivated the gentler among us, including our lone witness, John, who we ambushed as he passed by with Daisy. Bribed with hot chocolate, he agreed to perch briefly at a table as we demanded his opinion. He confessed a preference for this bird explanation. He seemed soothed by the notion that it must have been a far-off and long-dead person, not a local sufferer who lost the hand.

A tall dentist with a distracted air reminisced about the high white towers of India where certain Hindu sects expose their dead to be picked clean by birds. The dentist drank straight espresso from a paper cup as he stood rocking slowly from heel to toe in the shadow of a deep blue awning. He segued predictably to the

Tibetan method of disposing of the dead. He lingered over the impatience of the waiting vultures, hopping and flexing their wings and necks just out of reach of the priests who crush every bone and chop the corpse into bird-bite morsels on that wind-stripped plateau.

These reflections inspired John to tidy his side of the table, wipe a spill with his paper napkin, shove the napkin into his paper cup and rise with the cup and Daisy's leash in opposing hands. He was leaving again before I could ask him for details of the hand's appearance. Excusing himself, he tipped the empty cup in farewell before depositing it in the sidewalk waste bin.

The dentist took John's empty but still-warm chair to hear the Audubon volunteer explaining why the gull, having carried the hand so far, might abandon it. A midair attack, perhaps by a rival gull. Now that she thinks of it, there is a crow clan nesting in the taller firs in the park. She's seen crows ganging up on the local hawks to drive them away from the rookery.

Once dropped, the thing was quickly found at dawn there in the park amid the sleepers and joggers and walkers of dogs. The birdwatcher pictured the gull pacing at a distance, anxious to retrieve its titbit but stymied by gawking humans, harassed by diving crows.

A flurry of muttering from two tables down ended with one voice breaking out with the news that a bird wasn't absolutely necessary. There were other beasts.

The speaker had seen a whole family of opossums parade down an alley just the night before. Big Possum leading, then middle-sized followed by three identical kits, all in a row, tails high.

Several nods agreed that if the hand was misplaced at the

funeral home a possum could have carried it the short distance to the park.

Someone else proposed raccoons, reminding us of the noisy pair who play their shriek-and-chase games over the roofs and building marquees. Questions of raccoon and possum diets were raised and disputed.

Inevitably, the topic of rats surfaced. So close to the river and the docks, our rats are impressive and bold. Dark tales of rodent encounters followed, so it was a relief when one of the hill folk spoke up for coyotes.

The expensive-view houses on the hills behind us had been under siege for years. Too many reports of bloody cat fur smeared in the shrubbery or pooch carcasses gutted on front lawns meant the hill pets were kept locked indoors. On still nights even here on the low ground we hear coyotes yipping to each other up above.

Their range is much wider than the coons' and possums', of course. None of us was sure that a coyote couldn't or wouldn't carry a hand all the way down from the cemetery. We all laughed when somebody said coyotes were so smart they'd take a bus. It seemed close to true.

'You're forgetting the blood,' said a woman who had been so silent I hadn't noticed her. 'There was a trail of blood leading away on the sidewalk next to the grass. John said so.'

I don't know her but others at the table called her Margo. She had a weathered leopard face and a grey helmet of hair. Her voice was low, a courteous purr.

'The blood was liquid,' she said. 'It had to be fresh.'

She ignored us as she spoke, staring into the cup in front of her.

'Imagine,' she said, 'a homeless guy. A beggar and wine addict. He hurts his hand somehow, an accident, a fight. The bones are fractured and infection sets in. Or it's just a scratch from rooting in the garbage, from sliding through the brush at night looking for a place to curl up and sleep.

'But it doesn't heal. Blood poisoning, or staph infection, then gangrene. The pain is agonising. But there's a reason he summers under the bushes and winters in a crate beneath the railway bridge. He hates hospitals, doctors, police, social workers, all emblems of authority.

'He has a heavy knife. Maybe even a hatchet,' she said. 'He scrapes enough change for enough booze to bring his blood level to .307, the brink of unconsciousness. Then he hacks off the hand. He wraps a rag around the stump and staggers away. Or he persuades a booze buddy to do it for him.

'Picture two of them dressed in layers. Shirt over shirt over shirt. Their beards short and scraggly from poor nutrition. The hairs break off rather than growing in full. They are familiars of the street. We see them and look away. They squabble often, but stick together. The one injured and in pain. The pal offended by the growing smell of the wound, the delirium of the wounded, his cries in the dark.

'The friend takes less than his share of the bottle that night, so the wounded one will be stupefied. He wraps a belt in a tourniquet above the limp elbow as though they were going to shoot up. Well meaning, he props the arm against the metal of that meaningless sculpture. He waits for the steady snore. When he strikes, the blow is sharp and clean. He lifts the gasping, blinking body with anxious care and staggers away with him, or wheels him, rattling in their shared shopping cart. They are hiding somewhere in the neighbourhood. Some rarely visited basement or some stand of weeds abandoned at the end of an alley.

'Or maybe,' she said, 'the hand's owner has actually died by now from shock and blood loss. The friend has emptied the pockets, taken the shoes if they fit or are swappable, appropriated that valuable shopping cart or fled on a southbound freight as befits the lateness of the season.

'Maybe the corpse is lying one handed beneath a thin cover of leaves, or cardboard, or at the bottom of a dumpster. Maybe the dumpster has been emptied already into one of the huge trucks that shatter our sleep before dawn. Maybe his flaccid, colourless form is already deep in a landfill to be unearthed by some archaeologist of the future who will consider this one-handed skeletal remain a fair representative of our time, and of us.'

The tables were emptying before she finished. No one offered a comment but brisk head-shaking accompanied their caffeinated strides. She didn't seem surprised, just lifted her cup and looked into it.

As far as I know hers were the last words spoken on the subject of the hand. The intrigue died overnight. By the next morning the grocery clerks were rolling their eyes over a parking bribery scheme. The million topics of the population swept back to separate us. My own regrets have to do with the game ending just as I caught a faint glimmer of the rules. I say nothing, of course, only asking, as if casually, the names of certain dogs. Perhaps the others have not forgotten but are, like me, waiting to hear.

bull in the heather

scott mebus

Unlike most of the authors in this book, or the majority of you reading this right now, I actually don't know all that much about Sonic Youth. I love them in theory, of course. Who doesn't? But when it comes down to practising that love, I find I never really got around to it. I know that makes me a horribly uncool person, but being uncool has been my cross to bear for quite some time now, so I'm used to the pity. Only one Sonic Youth song can currently be found sitting forlornly in its own lonely playlist on my iPod. And that is the song whose title I have stolen for my story: 'Bull in the Heather'. Why? Because when it came out, I had never heard anything like it. I was a mainstream guy, and when this video popped up on my mainstream MTV, it was as if someone had slipped me a mickey. I was totally unprepared. I still hear the atonal chorus in that mocking female voice ringing through my head. It's annoying, and I kinda like it that way. So I carry the song with me, a little nugget of musical nonconformity intimidating the

*rest of my downloaded music with its bad attitude.
That's why I'm giving you a story that's a little
different from what I usually write. In honour of that
damn mocking voice that won't leave me be.*

|||||||||||||||||||||||||||||

Sue Carlyle was shopping for a penis. Not for herself, of course.
God knows she had no use for one. It was a gift. A little surprise for
her good friend Heather, a girl so beautiful it made her heart hurt.
Lately Sue had become increasingly worried that Heather might
be longing for one of those ridiculous creatures and, like the good
girlfriend she was, Sue was determined to give her baby what she
wanted. Not that Heather had come out and said anything, she was
too classy for that, but Sue prided herself on knowing her lover's
mind and over the past few weeks something was on it and Sue was
terrified it might be a penis. Hence the shopping trip.

Sue didn't know a thing about penises. She had never seen
one, not even her father's. She knew about the general shape from
seventh-grade health class and the graffiti on the subway, but
beyond that she was blind. She considered asking Ty, her make-up
artist, for a quick peek, just for a frame of reference, but neither of
them wanted that. So instead she decided to follow her usual game
plan when shopping (which she hated to do) and just hope for the
best and keep the receipt. She did ask Ty for some store suggestions
and he gladly sent her downtown to his favourite spot. But beyond
that, she was on her own.

She supposed this type of adventure would be best undertaken at night, but she had no patience for theatrics. So the sun hung high in the sky as Sue made her way down the narrow side streets of a part of town mostly asleep at this hour. She stumbled across Ty's store almost immediately; Wildly Suggestive, the sign above the window read in playful pink letters. Behind the glass beneath the sign a small scene had been arranged depicting a mannequin couple dressed in leather clothing directly opposed to their plastic genitalia (or lack thereof). The man/woman stood above the woman/man with a large vibrator in hand in what could be construed as a menacing gesture, if not for the total blank expressions on both their plastic faces. Instead, the effect was of an unorthodox Tupperware party right before the sale. Sue ignored the display, set her shoulders and stepped into the store.

The small space within overflowed with merchandise. The walls, already close, pushed bright red and pink boxes right up alongside her, each promising a transcendental sexual experience unachievable by organic means. Thin strips of gauzy material topped with limp plastic bows hung off hangers above her, threatening to melt off their wearer's body at the first touch of sweat. Over-endowed women in bottle-blonde hair struck lascivious poses on the walls, their lips bulging out like collagen blisters. Sue imagined Heather up on that wall, her features puffed up as if attacked by a sex-crazed Photoshop imager, her beautiful skin mummified in shiny black latex, her lovely dark hair drained of life and colour, her winsome face arranged into a clown's vision of lust. Was this what Heather missed? Being imagined like this? Being assaulted like this? Sue was out of her depth.

Sue moved farther into the store. Now the merchandise surrounding her began to replace crude photos with grinning cartoons. Sex became a joke as huge-breasted cartoon women peddled candy garters and cherry-flavoured edible condoms (a particularly senseless item, to her mind – how many babies came about because of that snack? she wondered). Small wind-up penises with large, improbable feet hopped about in front of boxes of breast-shaped pasta. 'Novelty' was the word plastered everywhere. Sue hated that word. Love was not light hearted; it was no game. Love was deep, so deep, and did not involve cartoons or wind-up toys or, least of all, novelty.

Sue pressed on. She began to feel like Lucy in the wardrobe as she walked forward with no end in sight. The merchandise took a dark turn and whips and chains appeared around her. Red balls to be lodged into the mouth of the willing lover hung above piles of sharp, cruel heels. Sue kept her eyes ahead and moved swiftly past.

Finally, the back of the store came into view. A small counter in the corner with a single beaten-up cash register stood next to a large case filled with what she had come to buy: penises. Rows and rows of penises. Was this the normal progression? she wondered to herself as she slowed to examine the items in the case. A too-quick journey that began with the promise of full lips and silky undergarments, and ended here among the dildos and vibrators? She didn't dwell on the thought; after all, this was not her place. She was here for a friend.

The vibrators were of no use to her. She had one herself, a small pink thing she'd been given at a bachelorette party a few years back. She'd succumbed to it once, with little effect. It made her uncomfortable to feel the cold plastic pressed up against her skin. The vibrations sucked the joy out of the sensations she sought. She hid the device deep in her closet. Heather had come upon it once when searching for a T-shirt. It made her giggle like a little girl. She danced around with it, waving it about like a magic wand, threatening to transform Sue's clitoris into a pumpkin. Sue laughed along, though inside she cringed. Heather recognised the make of the device and dismissed it as archaic. She had her own small crop of helpers and she offered to take Sue on a sampling tour. Sue couldn't decline quickly enough. It smacked of novelty.

Ignoring anything battery powered, Sue turned her attention to the dildos. They seemed so flimsy, so ineffective, that she couldn't understand the allure. What did Heather see in them? The thought of an answer made Sue's stomach roll.

Sue had met Heather at a publicity function. Sue was shooting for a trade paper while Heather was running the event: something to do with fashion designers dressing up their pets. Sue noticed Heather immediately; later they both noticed an inordinate number of photos with Heather's slim form just at the edge of the frame. But Sue held back. Heather proved extremely difficult to figure out; one moment she'd be letting her fingers linger in the hand of a beautiful redhead and Sue's spirits would soar. The next, she'd be whispering playfully into the ear of a well-built waiter and Sue's world would crash. As a rule Sue avoided fence sitters; though beautiful, they did the digestion no favours. But something about this girl stuck with her and she kept her just at the edge of the frame.

Towards the end of the evening, Sue decided she'd taken enough photos to satisfy her employer and reached for her lens cap. It fell from her hand and came to rest against a beautiful open-toe shoe. A delicate hand reached down, lifted the cap and carried it up to its owner. Sue met Heather's gaze as Heather dropped the cap into her hand. Heather's smile told Sue that she'd noticed the attention, even as her eyes didn't know how to feel about it. Against her better judgement, Sue invited Heather to dinner. Two dinners, a coffee and a breakfast later they were lovers.

Heather had never been with a woman. She'd spent her thirty years bouncing from man to man without thought; easily hopping on to a new boat just as the last one sank. Some treated her poorly, others well. None of it excited her any more, she confided to Sue, as they lay intertwined. But this was different. Sue brought something to Heather's life none of those poor men could ever hope to provide: understanding. Sue understood her baby. She knew how things should feel. Heather had never been happier and neither had Sue. Something deep grew between them, something true. And now, eight months later, Sue stood in the back of a dingy little sex store staring at rubber penises. That was the price of love.

'Can I help you?'

Sue practically jumped out of her skin, though outwardly she seemed only to blink and turn at the voice. A young boy, no older than eighteen, had come out from the back to stand behind the counter. He had thin, stringy hair and watery eyes that sank downwards beneath Sue's stare. This was men, she thought.

'Are these all the... aids you have?' she asked.

'We've got some others in the back,' he replied, looking a little below her and to the right. 'You wanna seem 'em?'

'Not yet,' she replied. 'I'm still browsing.'

She turned back to the case. Her heart beat so loud that she felt sure the boy could hear it, but he gave no sign. Her hands began to sweat as she felt the boy's eyes, now freed from her strong gaze, land upon her back. As she always did in stressful times, she took charge.

'Are all the dildos like these?' Her voice rang with authority.

'What do you mean?' the boy asked, a small crack appearing at the end of the sentence.

'This flimsy, I mean.'

'No. We got glass ones over here. They're real sturdy.' He pointed to a trio of icicles standing in the corner of the case.

'Don't they get cold?'

'I guess.' The boy blushed. People usually purchased or they left. They didn't ask questions. 'I wouldn't know.'

'What's this?' She pointed to a long, rubbery snake with twin heads.

'That's for… well… both a' ya.'

'Ah.' She nodded. 'A double-sided dildo. I've heard of these. It doesn't look satisfying.'

'I guess not.'

'How close to a real penis would you rate these things?' she asked smoothly, though inside she reeled and tumbled with shame.

'Well…' The boy did not want to answer this question. 'Not too close, I guess.'

'I want realism,' she declared.

'Um, I guess that you could maybe look at a strap-on. They look pretty real.'

This threw Sue worse than the boy's first appearance. She strove to keep the waters still.

'Of course! I should have guessed. Bring me your most realistic strap-on.' He slunk away to the back, happy to run. Sue stood rigid in place, waiting. She'd heard of strap-ons, of course. She'd never wished to be acquainted with one. But this seemed a step in the right direction. If she wished to push the thought of penises from

Heather's mind, then appropriating the image would be the way to go. She could be like any man, but no man could be like her.

The boy returned, a long box in hand. He smiled nervously as he opened it.

'It's called the Bull. It's the only kind we got that looks real, cause it's from a mould, it says. A real porn star di... um, penis. Iron Jeremy. Heard of him?'

Sue stared at him coldly until his weak smile dissolved.

'No, I haven't.'

The boy swallowed and returned to opening the box. The picture on the front seemed promising. Long and thick, with actual veins running up and down the shaft, it certainly appeared anatomical. It looked much firmer than the dildos in the case. Hopefully it wouldn't remind Heather of a previous lover, at least not one in particular. Sue's stomach began to ease as she warmed to the idea.

'Sorry it's takin' so long, the harness is all tangled up,' the boy said quickly, fumbling inside the package. 'It's real nice. Silicone based, and it warms up so you don't have to worry about the cold. It's the only strap-on I'd use... If I used one, you know? We only have a few left. It should do you fine... Here you go...'

His voice trailed off as he pulled it out and he let out a spastic giggle at what he saw. Sue's stomach dropped and her voice took on its most authoritative tone yet.

'You must have another.'

The boy nodded and quickly ran into the back, leaving the large thing lying stiff on the counter for Sue to contemplate. There had to be another. The boy returned.

'That's the only version of that type we have left, lady,' he said, miserable under her hard stare. 'I'm sorry.'

'When does your next shipment arrive?'

'Not till next month. You can try our sister store in Brooklyn if you want, though I think they'll say the same.'

There was no chance of repeating this experience, she thought silently. As she stared at the shaft lying on the counter, she considered her options. It was a penis, after all. One penis was as good as another, right? Once strapped on, it would be the picture of reality, almost. This was what Heather wanted. Sue had to show her that there was nothing that she couldn't provide her with. Be it a vacation in the Hamptons, a loving, understanding ear, or a large, erect member, it all came from Sue. Anyway, wasn't it the size that mattered? She was sure she'd heard that somewhere. The truth was, she couldn't wait a month. She needed to do this now, before it was too late. Heather teetered and Sue had to push in the right direction.

'I'll take it.'

The boy swallowed and quickly stuffed the thing back into its box. Sue paid, grabbed her package and then walked with dignity and no small amount of speed past the whips and chains, the hopping penises and breast-shaped pasta, the cheap negligees and the leering faces of the women on the walls, out the door and away.

Heather had come home distracted again, and this time Sue joined her as they ate in silence. Afterwards Sue implored her to wait in the bedroom with eyes closed for a special surprise. Heather cried weariness, but Sue was insistent. This was a special gift, just for you, she said. Just for my baby. Heather waited in the bedroom now, eyes shut, uncertain what Sue had in store. Sue stood in the bathroom, naked, her pale white skin glowing under the harsh light.

Heather could tan without trying but Sue only burned. She pulled out the penis and attached it to her pelvis. It wasn't complicated and she'd already read the instructions ten times. After a moment, it was done. Her penis hung from her like a bloated cocoon about to let loose a butterfly. It felt heavy around her waist. She hoped it looked real, or real enough. A small flash of worry, the last she would entertain, raced through her. If only they'd had another colour. It was so… black. It seemed even blacker against her pale skin than she'd anticipated in the store. Glancing in the mirror, she took in the two-toned creature with the long black tube growing out of her crotch and a small voice whispered to her that she appeared thrown together, a sexual Frankenstein. But she pushed that voice away. Maybe that's what all penises are: hanging flesh both ugly and ridiculous, practically unnatural. She'd never understand. She took it in her hand. It did feel strong. Big, black and strong. She mastered herself. This would be a good night.

'Keep them closed, baby. Wait till you see what I have for you!' she said through the door. Adjusting the brand-new penis at her waist, she took a deep breath and prepared to make her baby happy.

shadow of a doubt

rebecca godfrey

Kim's voice is somehow both menacing and alluring in this song. I always loved how she sang the words so they were less like lyrics, and more like a mystery. The song could be a girl's whispered confession or a taunting denial. It could be both. You're never really sure, but you want to keep on listening.

|||||||||||||||||||||||||||||||||||

This is a story I never told the police. I'm telling you because you're not a cop. You probably read all my statements, right? I got dragged in by the cops yesterday, and I told them what I know because I do believe Teri should get in trouble for what she did to the deaf girl. I really do. A lot of kids at my school think we shouldn't say anything because even if Teri killed that girl, she was probably really high and, at the end of the day, she's one of us. The thing is I've known Teri my whole life. She used to be my best friend. That's why I came to you because I heard you're writing a book about the murder. I think that's weird, to tell you the truth. Why would somebody from

New York want to write a book about us? You must have so many murders in New York. And me and my friends, we're just nobodies in this world. You must be bored hanging out in Walton. Anyway, I never told the cops this story.

Can you turn your tape recorder off? I don't mean to be rude but machines make me nervous, and yours is so small; it looks like a black eye. You remind me so much of my sister except she has more tattoos. She has twenty-seven. She got her first one when she was twelve. Have you talked to Colby Straith? You have, right? Yeah, he told me he talked to the lady from New York. I hope you don't trust that guy because the thing is he's kind of a rapist. If anyone should be in jail, it's Colby fucking Straith 'cause when my sister was twelve, her and all those roughneck girls, the whole C-Town crew, they would go to Colby for tattoos, but he would just, well, you know, he said it was fair trade. My sister hates her first tattoo now, but what can you do? She's got that star for life. You *really* look like her, though. Your eyes move in the same way. I think that's why I trust you. Some people think you're a narc. They think you're working for the cops. I'm serious. Your face looks so funny right now. You just looked away from me and right down at your fancy tape recorder. You turned it off, right? I really hope you're not a cop because what I'm about to tell you is private and crazy. Slade said he doesn't think you are a cop because when he was in your hotel room he snooped around while you were in the bathroom. He said you had a whole shitload of pills from a pharmacy in New York City. I guess you caught him, right? And you told him the pills were for headaches, but he looked them up on the Internet and he said they were for anxiety. I really like your ring.

A long time ago, two summers ago, all I wanted to do was die. I was very suicidal. The priest told me to think of the darkness like a black bird and let it fly out of my body. Can you believe that? For a while, I tried to feel better by remembering the day I was most happy and that was a day when I was twelve and my dad was still alive. We were in the canoe over by Candle Island and I reached down and touched this whale that was moving through the waves and that dark place in the water, the part where the whale rose up, was right under my palm and my dad kept quiet and let the oars lie still and our boat just floated for a long time while we watched the whale in those waves far away.

I should let you know that a lot of people are lying to you, telling you bullshit stories about Teri, not because they're bad people, but I guess they want to be in a book. They think they might get famous or something. I'm not like that, though. I just think someone should know about what happened with me and Teri.

We were with Eliza. The three of us used to skip school and hang out by the train tracks over on Chatham Hill. This was when we were thirteen. Do you know Eliza? Some people call her Lizzy. She has thin eyebrows and her hair's bleached pure blonde. I heard she took off and she's missing and she's gone into hiding ever since Teri got arrested. I doubt she gave a statement because when Matty Hargrove got arrested she said she wasn't a rat and she asked the cops if she looked like she had a tail. She lies sometimes, Eliza. She says she's a model but she's never been in magazines. Anyway, we were by the train tracks because we used to go there to get away from everyone.

Teri said to Eliza: 'Arielle wants to die, so today we're going to help her.'

Teri has this way about her. You believe she knows best. I did what she said. She told me to go lie down on the tracks and I did. I walked over to the tracks and I laid myself down in the low place. As soon as I lay down, five crows flew out of a tree and passed above, right above me. The rust was cold on my ankles; I could feel the old rain; the saved rain; all the old, saved rain under my body. The train was still far away and I was not scared. I'm finally doing what I should be doing. I'm finally giving up caring. I was almost happy because soon I would see my father.

Waiting for my death might have been peaceful except Teri got so angry at Eliza. I've seen her when she's vicious but never as she was that afternoon. Teri's so small and that's why some people don't think she could have killed the deaf girl but I've known her my whole life and she can have this fury. She went crazy because Eliza was being dreamy and not watching me. Eliza sometimes is in her own world, as if the sky is a mirror or the dirt is a catwalk. She walks; one hand on her hips; she turns. Teri's yelling, 'This is going to be fun. Watch!' And I guess that's when Eliza saw me, waiting for my suicide.

Eliza yells, 'Get off the tracks!' She's like, 'Ari! Get off the tracks!' I think I heard the train. And Teri moves closer to me. She comes right up to me. She whispers. She touches my forehead. She says, 'Just stay there. You want to kill yourself, don't you? Just stay there. Stay where you are.'

Teri said she was really proud of me. I looked towards her to say goodbye and she had this smile on her face. She was kneeling in the long grass, smoking a cigarette, with this smile I did not like. It reminded me of the look on Colby's face right after he gave my sister that tattoo. It's like they've taken something, not like a thief, but like a winner who's cheated. Oh, I can't explain. I heard the train. The train was coming. I heard the rumble, the wheels in all the dirt and gravel. And I tried to be good, to be ready, to do what I wanted which when I was thirteen was only and always to die. I thought of my sister and how she played her radio at night; the sound I could sometimes hear; just sometimes her singing; her little voice in the bedroom; and after my dad died, she'd move the radio to the wall between us, and sing louder because she didn't want me to hear her tears, I guess, or she wanted me not to be alone with the air and the silence.

There was so much rain underneath me on the tracks. I could feel the breath of the train and smell the coal. I heard the rumbled noise getting closer to me and I was wondering if there was a man in front of the train, a driver, who might see me because I know those coal trains have no captains or passengers. I heard Teri say, 'Good girl. Stay still.' And then I thought it was her hand but it was Eliza and she was just above me and beside me and she was pulling me and grabbing my shoulders and Teri just started pounding on Eliza's back, just whacking her and Eliza's white hair was like lightning. She was just being flung around and Teri is screaming. She's yelling, 'Eliza! Get off her. Leave her alone! She *wants* to die! Let her die!'

I was so dizzy when I stumbled over the rails. Eliza pulled me towards the grass and I could feel her tears and the ground trembled a little when the train passed us by. We just lay there crying and dizzied and shivering. Teri threw her cigarette into the grass and she spoke to me so coldly. She hated me more than she's ever hated any girl in Walton. 'Arielle,' she said. 'I thought you told me you wanted to die.'

'Well, not like that, I guess.' That's what I told her, almost like an apology, but she just left me and I remember she walked away on the tracks, kind of showing off, I think, that she could balance on the edge and not lie down on the rain. She always had this way to make me feel ashamed. I felt like I was the one who had done the wrong mistake and I almost ran after her to tell her I was sorry. Eliza kept saying, 'She would have let you do it. She would have just walked away.' I didn't want to talk about it because Teri was my best friend. But Eliza kept talking about it and she would not stop. She's like, 'You know what? Teri would have just gone home, and been almost happy, saying, "Oh, Arielle committed suicide!"' A week or so later, when we were in English, Teri told me she was just joking around and she was trying to save me. She said she was using reverse psychology.

Have you seen Eliza? You should ask her about that day. She might not want to talk about it to you because, in this town, people like to forget the terrible things. It's that way, already, with the deaf girl. Nobody calls her by her real name. And they never say murder or stabbing. They just say, 'That thing that happened by the river.' Same with the cops. They kept asking me about 'the incident'. I got a little mouthy with them, which they didn't appreciate. I said, 'I don't know why you use words like *incident* when a girl my age was stabbed.' I hope you don't use the word incident in your book but I guess that's pretty much your choice.

Do you know Teri's mother? I saw her yesterday coming out of the Safeway. She was just pushing her cart in this frail way. She always seems faint, almost as if she's been faded out or rubbed away. She told me Teri's just a scapegoat and we're all the bad girls who messed up her good and kind daughter. She said she got a big lawyer for Teri and the lawyer told her all about the dead girl and how she kept a diary and wrote about how she wanted to be reincarnated, or something, go to the other side. After Teri's mom yelled at me, I had to go back to school and it's been so hard to concentrate. I keep wondering how Teri had all that power with me. Do you know? If you met Teri, she'd probably convince you she was right about the whole world, even if you are from New York City.

I'm sorry but can you please not put this story in your book. It's not that I think you're a narc. I just decided I do not want anyone to know this story. Please promise me. You could give me a different name? I guess that would be all right, but not really, because even if you changed my name everybody will know it's me because I'm the only one in this town with red hair who lives by the railroad and has a father who died so suddenly when he woke up with his heart closed, just closed, like a broken clock, the doctors said, like a wrongly tied wire.

flower

steven sherrill

'Use the word: fuck. The word is love.' I mean, come on... is there any human endeavour or struggle that doesn't have its knotty roots spread out in the space between those two words? The older I get, the less I know. How the hell did Sonic Youth figure things out so early?

||||||||||||||||||||||||||||||||

Sitting in the waiting room of Tommy's Tyre Town, with late February, 5 p.m., and the ash-grey sleet that incessantly peppered the wall of windows all conspiring to obliterate any shred of hope and good cheer, Ulla Shooks wished she could kick off her thick-soled shoes and rub some cream into her bunions. After a forty-hour work week, dishing up pot-pie and lasagna, mushy green beans and flavourless corn kernels, after five shifts of keeping the chopped eggs, the croutons, the mixed lettuces and all the other stainless steel bins on the Saving Grace Hospital cafeteria salad bar full, everything ached. And the pain – like her heavy hips, her sixty-year-old breasts, her sagging cheeks and wattled neck – the pain, too, seemed at the mercy of gravity. It settled mostly in her feet.

Ulla Shooks sat with her back to the other wall of windows, the one offering an unabashed view of the three men at work in the two garage bays. She didn't want to see it. Any of it. Their grease-smeared faces, their cigarettes, their ill-fitting blue uniforms: one hanging loosely from a scarecrow of a man whose skin was so pale he'd be invisible if not for the oily stains; the other not quite containing the belly, neck or arms of the crew chief, a mopey man who could easily be either thirty or fifty years old; and Tommy, whose shirt might actually fit should he ever decide to tuck it in.

For more reasons than even she was aware of, Ulla couldn't bear willing witness to the activities in the garage. And even though the air wrench's harsh ratchet startled her, sent a jolt up and down her spine every single time one of the men tightened or loosened a lug nut, she preferred to look the other way, out the other windows where the view offered up the Long John Silver parking lot, Plank Road and, somewhere through the thick winter clouds, Tussey Mountain.

And if the placement of the flickering television (perched on a plywood shelf near the ceiling in the far corner in the direction of the unseeable mountains) was any indication, the mechanics didn't want her watching them anyway. Ulla would've gladly watched the broadcasted game show, despite the jagged bolts of static that shot across the TV screen each time the air wrenches fired; would've found comforting distraction in the too-excited cheers from the audience and in the charming wit of the impeccably haired host. Would've enjoyed these, but couldn't because the only other waiting customer in the lobby kept pacing back and forth between his chair, right beneath the television, and the high counter by the door to the garage, muttering to himself about how much time he was wasting.

Rude. Inconsiderate. Ulla wasn't about to look, but she felt sure this man, with his fancy tie and his clean fingernails, probably drove a pricey Japanese car. Something garishly coloured. It would not have occurred to her to rush the service on her ageing Ford Taurus. Patience does a body good: human or automobile.

By the time the man had paid and left, the game show had ended in a frenetic chorus of shrieks and palpably urgent music. In its place, the local news promised details and regular updates on a breaking story about a stand-off at the city's animal shelter. Ulla, not tall enough to reach the volume or channel buttons on the television itself, half-heartedly looked around for a remote. Truth was, even if she'd found it, and even though she was the only person in the room, changing the channel without Tommy's OK went against her nature.

Ulla riffled through the stacks of magazines on the low, flimsy and only table in the waiting room. *Auto Week. Popular Science. Modern Turkey Hunter. Sports Illustrated.* Nothing provided for the gentler gender but a single coverless *Woman's Day*, and it two years old. More out of obligation than interest, Ulla picked up the magazine and flipped to the table of contents, not at all surprised to find not one, not two but three different articles on the topic of sex. One a survey, one a how-to and the third too disgusting to even finish reading the title. And in *Woman's Day*, of all places. Ulla clucked her tongue and slipped the magazine to the bottom of a stack.

Turning her head only as far as necessary to catch a glimpse of the big clock behind the counter – its hands made of polished wrenches, miniature pictures of tyres, oil cans and various other automobile images made up the numbers – as best she could tell, Ulla determined it to be 5.30. No hurries. Nobody to get home to. Nothing going on at church. But Lord have mercy, her feet hurt. She'd have liked nothing more than to slip out of those tight, black shoes and prop her feet on the table until her car was ready. But under no conceivable circumstances would Ulla Shooks sacrifice decorum for comfort. No. She'd settle for the small, small comfort of knowing she did the right thing.

Ulla reached into her serviceable purse and plucked out the newest issue of *Hark!*, the Riggle's Gap First Congregation Church of the Brethren's biweekly bulletin, and began reading closely over the lists of deaths, births, calls for prayer, admonitions and aphorisms, and one or two good-natured, clean jokes. Ulla took care to turn the pages of the centre-stapled, single-fold publication by their corners to avoid the easily smudged ink. While she had no official editorial role, Ulla felt sure that her efforts towards pointing out typos and grammatical errors were appreciated by the higher-ups.

Five thirty. Her feet hurt. And the wind-driven sleet tapped an unending, erratic beat against the glass. Ulla had a headache. Probably from the various fumes she smelled wafting from the garage. She couldn't concentrate on the issue of *Hark!*, but wasn't ready to concede defeat. Ulla took her glasses off and pinched the bridge of her nose. Anyone passing by on Plank Road, anyone who took the time to slow down, anyone able to penetrate the night, the storm, and peer into the fluorescent-lit diorama that was the waiting room of Tommy's Tyre Town, would've thought Ulla Shooks was praying as she sat there. Or weeping.

Who could've guessed that she was indulging in her one decadent fantasy?

'Miss Shooks! Miss Shooks!' All the fifth-graders cried out excitedly. *'Tell us again about the wicked old comma splice!'* They flock around her, the boys, the girls, their eager pencils clutched tight. *'Miss Shooks! Tell us what happened to the boy who put e before i!'*

'Miss Shooks.'

A bell. The door?

'Miss Shooks?'

Ulla clutched at the copy of *Hark!* She must've closed her eyes. Must've dozed off. It wasn't her imaginary students calling her name. It was Tommy, standing, untucked, directly in front of her, clicking a ballpoint pen against a clipboard.

'Speed-balancing, Miss Shooks?'

'Excuse me?' Ulla said.

With the pen, Tommy pointed towards the counter, but he looked in the direction of the new customer.

'You want me to speed-balance them wheels?'

Ulla looked at Tommy, then at the girl standing in the middle of the room, then at her own weary feet. She had no idea what 'speed-balancing' meant.

'Why, yes,' she said to Tommy. 'That'd be real nice.'

Tommy scribbled something on the clipboard then stepped behind the counter, where he, and Ulla from her seat, stared at the girl. The girl.

The girl stood, her booted feet (scuffed black lineman's boots, laced up to mid-calf) planted wide, her mangy thrift-store faux-fur coat hanging nearly to her ankles, but open enough for anyone to read her Hunka-Hunka-Burnin-Luv T-shirt, the text arcing over and under the mounds (and even Ulla could see that they were mounded) of breasts, the coat open enough for anyone willing to look at the wide crescent of pale flesh where the hems of her shirt and skirt didn't quite meet, the dark pucker of her navel, the shiny gold barbell piercing it, stood with her hands plunged deep into the coat pockets, stood with her mouth open, another gold ball fixed in her tongue and clicking against her teeth, with her black-lined eyes shut, stood with the melting pellets of sleet glistening like diamonds in her hair, on her collar, stood swaying and bobbing her head in time with a bass beat that even Ulla and Tommy could hear pulsing from the girl's earphones.

'Can I help you, ma'am?'

Then louder.

'Can I help you, ma'am?!'

When the girl opened her eyes, Ulla forced her attention back to *Hark!*, and worked hard to keep it there as the girl shuffled over to the counter to negotiate with Tommy.

'Ya'll sell retreads?'

Ulla wanted to look. She could hear the girl's music. She could hear Tommy's ballpoint pen clicking and clicking.

'No, ma'am,' Tommy said. 'We don't carry retreads.'

'You don't got any retreads?' the girl asked, with a shift in her tone.

Ulla couldn't help herself, she had to look, to see whether that young hussy had leaned in and perched those breasts on Tommy's counter, which she had, but Tommy, to his credit, would not be moved.

'No, ma'am. We don't carry retreads.'

'What's the cheapest tyres you got?' she asked, the syllables punctuated by the click of metal against her teeth.

'What kind of car is it?' Tommy asked.

The girl pointed into the parking lot, into the night, and both Tommy and Ulla looked.

'That old Ford Taurus out there,' she said.

Tommy sucked some air through his teeth. Ulla felt he was giving the girl's question too much thought. Too much importance. Ulla felt the best thing would be for Tommy to send the girl on down the road, to some other more appropriate tyre store, one with a different clientele.

Tommy flipped open a thick binder.

'I can do these for forty-five dollars apiece, but that don't include speed-balancing.'

The girl asked if she could get just one.

'No, ma'am,' he said. 'Wouldn't be safe. But I can do your front two.'

'OK, then,' she said.

'Be about half an hour.'

Tommy eased back into the garage. The girl went into the unisex bathroom opposite the counter. Ulla could still hear her music, even through the closed door. Ulla thought she heard the girl singing. Ulla most certainly heard the unregulated stream of urine, and clearly heard neither a flush, nor water in the sink. Ulla said a little prayer that the girl would wait outside for her tyres. Or maybe go eat at Long John Silver's.

But sometimes the Lord likes to test his followers.

The girl sat directly opposite Ulla. Directly. Not even one chair to the right or left.

Ulla held *Hark!* as high as she could without seeming too obvious, peered over its hard edge once or twice and determined that it didn't matter because the girl still had her eyes shut.

Had her head leaned back against the window, rolling rhythmically from side to side. Bump, bump, bumping the glass for percussive emphasis. Over the girl's shoulder, night had turned the window into a mirror. Ulla saw her own reflection – checked her posture – and beyond, in reverse, and incrementally smaller, Tommy and the other men in the garage, who'd paused in their work to gawk at the splay-legged girl sitting across the room, with her eyes closed, bobbing to music and fingering the stud in her navel. Clear as day, Ulla could see them! They stood right behind her, just on the other side of the glass, lined up like Christ and the two thieves at Calvary.

Shame. Shame on them all.

Mercifully, their voyeurism was brief.

Mercifully, the poor girl never knew.

She was too immersed in the song. The song she began to sing. Well, maybe *sing* wasn't the right word. The girl began to speak the lyrics of the song. Erratically. Partially garbled, but forceful nonetheless.

'There's a new girl in your life. Long red wavy hair. Green green lips and purple eyes. Skinny hips and big brown breasts...'

Oh dear Lord, she was singing about breasts! Ulla looked again for the television remote. Ulla looked towards the Long John Silver's sign, an improbable beacon in the distance.

'Support the power of women. Use the power of man. Support the flower of women...'

Surely, Tommy must be just about done. *Surely.* Surely, the girl won't keep singing about breasts in public. Surely, the Lord wants Ulla to learn something from this.

'Use the word: fuck!'

What? Surely, Ulla must've misheard.

'The word is love.'

The girl spoke, sang. Sang louder with each verse.

'Support the power of women. Use the power of man. Support the flower of women. Use the word: fuck! The word is love.'

Ulla stuffed her church bulletin into her purse, clutched the purse to her chest, like a lifejacket. A flotation device. She tried to pray, but found her silent words supplanted by the girl's song.

'Use the word: fuck!'

Ulla cleared her throat. Maybe the girl just didn't know she was singing aloud.

'The word is love. Use the power of women. Use the word...'

Ulla closed her eyes, but it didn't help. The air wrenches wailed behind her; across the narrow lobby, the girl sang her nasty song. Song. Yes! The Lord surely meant for Ulla to stand firm in this hard moment. To witness. To testify. To counter the wicked with the godly. Ulla knew what to do.

Ulla began to sing.

'Have you been to Jesus for the cleansing power?'

Ulla threw herself into the song, wavering briefly in and out of tune before finding her key.

'Are you washed in the blood of the Lamb? Are you fully trusting in his grace this hour?'

And the girl:

'Fuck! The word is love. Use the word.'

And Ulla:

'Are you washed in the blood of the Lamb? Are you washed (are you washed) in the blood (in the blood)?'

'Support the power of women. Use the power of man. Support the flower of women.'

'In the soul-cleansing blood of the Lamb. Are your garments spotless? Are they white as snow? Are you washed in the blood of the Lamb? Are you walking daily by the Saviour's side? Do you rest each moment in the Crucified?'

And still, she could hear the girl.

'Use the word: fuck! Use the word: fuck!'

So Ulla sang louder.

'Are you washed in the blood of the Lamb? When the Bridegroom cometh will your robes be white, pure and white in the blood of the Lamb?'

'Miss Shooks?'

'Will your soul be ready for the mansion bright? Are you washed in the blood of the Lamb?'

'Miss Shooks?'

'Lay aside the garments that are stained with sin, and be washed in the blood of the Lamb. There's a fountain flowing for the soul unclean. Oh, be washed in the blood of the Lamb!'

''Scuse me, Miss Shooks.'

Ulla Shooks opened her eyes after that final emphatic refrain, found Tommy and his clipboard standing, once again, directly in front of her. In the gap between his belly and crooked arm, Ulla could see the girl, open eyed and smiling in her direction.

'You're all done, Miss Shooks. I've got your bill ready.'

Ulla felt the shame crawl up her neck, felt her ears burn red.

She refused to look in the girl's direction. She gathered up her purse and followed Tommy to the counter, where he circled the total on her bill.

'You get free rotation after three thousand miles,' he said.

Ulla just nodded, dug into her bag for the chequebook.

The telephone rang and Tommy answered it, stretching the long cord back into the garage. Ulla printed out the name of the business and the amount on the plain green cheque in careful letters. She tore the cheque from its pad and when she slipped it under the paper clip on her own bill, Ulla saw the girl's invoice.

The girl.

Ulla tried to see the girl, reflected in the window, but couldn't. Heard her, though, another song pulsing harshly from the headphones. And more singing.

'Don't just stare, 'cause she's not wearing underwear, em-em-em-em-em-em-em-em...'

Ulla located the total on the young girl's bill, the charge for two cheap tyres, without speed-balancing. On a scrap of paper, she added that figure to itself, added another fifty dollars which she hoped would cover the speed-balancing.

'Oh, how rude, at least she's got your attention, square. Em-em-em-em-em-em-em-em...'

Almost hastily, Ulla wrote out the cheque for that calculated amount, clipped it to the girl's bill, scored out the 2 under Quantity. Wrote 4, and circled it. Wrote beneath, 'plus speed-balancing'.

'Don't you realise, it's just her disguise, ai-ai-ai-ai-ai-ai-ai-ai, hey mum! Look, no more panty line, ai-ai-ai-ai-ai-ai-ai-ai, shoewa

shoewa shoewa shoewa shoewa shoewa shoewa, i-i-i-i-i-i-i-i-i-i-i
-i-i-i-i-i-i-i-i-i-i-i-i-i-i-i-i-i-i…'

Ulla left Tommy's Tyre Town. The sleet had stopped. And wasn't
that the moon climbing up over Tussey Mountain?

wish fulfillment

mary gaitskill

*'Wish Fulfillment' isn't the best Sonic Youth song;
it's not even my favourite Sonic Youth song. But it's
the one that caught me when I was falling, years ago,
falling through the trapdoor in my living-room floor
many years ago. I fell into the song and found myself
walking down a corridor of slow sound, longing, with
all these pictures that I could only half see flying by.
When I play the song now, I can still see the corridor,
remember walking, and think I might find it again
one day. But I probably won't.*

One night Mary, a little girl with sisters and parents who loved her,
woke in a dark forest. At first she was afraid and then she realised
it was her backyard. During the day she sometimes pretended her
backyard was a forest and now, in the dream world of night, it had
become a forest. During the day she pretended there was a door
on the floor of the forest, and so now she went to look for it. She

found it between the garage and the fishpond, and she opened it with excitement and a little fear. During the day she had imagined that under the trapdoor there was a staircase lit with lamps, and so there was. Knowing by now that she was dreaming and that this chance might never come again, she went down the stairs, closing the door behind her.

As Mary descended the stairs, she became me, or, to put it another way, I became dimly aware of her, descending down into herself as I, a middle-aged woman, drove through the town where I live on a rainy spring night listening to an old song on an obsolete tape. The music in the song started with the sound of a crippled machine stripped to its barest function, turning unevenly round and round on a cockeyed pivot, screeching sweetly and brokenly. There was a sound like slow-struck bells and a voice like that of somebody looking for something in the dark. I used to listen to it years ago, lying drunk on my floor in the dark. I would listen and think of a woman I loved, or tried to love. Her name was Karen. We did not belong in the same world, but somehow our separate worlds had overlapped. *I see your wishes on the wall.* Karen was overspilling with impossible wishes and so was I. Our wishes were glowing, and always out of reach; they made life around us blurred, magical and painful. Our wishes were not the same at all, but somehow, we had met in the dark and, for a moment, our wishes had overlapped.

Meanwhile, the dreaming little girl named Mary continued down the stairs in the dark. Outside the glowing perimeters of lamplight, the dark was deep and physical. As she walked, a voice spoke. She could not tell whether it came from inside her or outside. It said: Now you must choose. You can keep going down and visit the Devil. Or you can stop on the landing and visit life on earth. Mary said aloud, 'I choose life on earth.' And she came to the landing. The landing was an enormous room, luxuriantly carpeted with nice little tables and chairs placed at intervals. There were pictures on the wall, and they were like paintings and movies combined; the figures in them were loosely formed like the figures in paintings and yet as defined and mobile as the characters in movies. In one of them a child looked out the window at a beautiful woman in the sky and longed for her. Music played; it was like the grinding of a machine with a personality, a personality that was sad and sweet and had to grind the same way over and over. The singer sang, and Mary understood the song to be a song of the child's longing – ancient longing that had taken new life in the body of the child. Mary looked at another picture; in that one a musician and a beautiful model kissed each other on the street at night, outside a bar called 'The White Rose'. They were like little pieces of glitter in human form, and they were sad because they knew that the lifespan of glitter is not as long as the lifespan of humans – that they would die shortly and yet be forced to live on in the body of a dull, sore human being for years after. The music was singing of their sadness, too.

The windshield wipers rub back and forth, bearing rippling streams of wet light. The wet windshield catches the lights of stores and street lamps and, for a second, I glimpse, between reflections of drugstore and laundromat lights, the reflection of something that has accidentally shown itself long enough for me to see its bright silhouette. *I see you run to make a call, putting up to someone free.* Far away and hard to see, Karen runs for the phone in a forgotten room down a long, long hall that twists and turns through a house with hundreds of rooms in it. I am in another room now, and in this room the song is about another person. It is about a girl, a poor girl named Kassandra. She came to me through charity. She came to stay with me in the summer. I was supposed to help her; I wanted to help her. Her mother was cruel and she was wishing for a new mother. I had no children and I was wishing for a daughter. We came from different worlds, and each of us spoke languages the other did not know, but still, for a while, our wishes overlapped.

On the luxuriant, carpeted landing, the little girl named Mary looks at another picture. In this one a dark, beautiful girl some years older than her is sitting on a bed in a dingy room, looking at wishes. In the picture, Mary can see the girl's wishes; they are wonderful and terrible. She wishes she was not poor. She does not know she is beautiful and so she wishes she was beautiful. She wishes she was a queen, more powerful and perfect than anybody, telling everybody what to do. She wishes to lay treasures at her mother's feet. She wishes to chop off her mother's head and put it in a goldfish bowl. She wishes to ride horses. She wishes she would be adopted by a woman who has money, who would love her and buy her things. Mary can feel the girl who sits on her poor bed, wishing and being pulled apart by the power of her longing. Mary can almost see the woman with money; she is pale and worried and she is going back and forth from young to old very fast. During one flash of youth, Mary realises that the woman with money is her.

There is the sound of bells; Mary is distracted and forgets what she realised. The picture of the beautiful dark girl becomes a picture of ringing bells; a big iron bell high up in a stone church; handbells rung by town criers; the electronic bell of a phone; the digital bell of a cell phone. The bells vanish. The girl is on her cell phone, but the person she is trying to call isn't there.

The phone is ringing. *Your life and my life, they don't touch at all/And that's no way to be.* I am home, turning on the lights, trying to get to the phone. The music continues in my head. *We've never seemed so far.* I bought Kassandra clothes and helped her with school twice a week on the phone. The other poor girls beat her because they were angry at her for having good clothes. They mocked her for doing better in school. Her mother mocked her too. And so she stopped calling me for help. She put the clothes I gave her in the bottom drawer.

The caller hangs up as I pick up. *We've never seemed so far.*

When Kassandra was ten years old I would read to her at bedtime. She would look at me with big glowing eyes, golden with wishes that overlapped with mine. I wished her to be a success. I wished her to be a champion horse rider. I wished her to grow up beautiful. I wished her surrounded by jewels.

The little girl named Mary is looking at a painting of the dark girl and the pale woman; the woman is holding the girl, and, even though she is the smaller of the two, she is able to hold her all the way. 'Your weight feels good to me,' she says. 'Lay on me all the way.' And the dark girl does.

Now Kassandra is following her dreams in the street among louche criminals, but I know her wishes are still golden and glowing. Our wishes no longer overlap – but they do. I know they do because sometimes when I am sick with sadness I feel her at my side with her hand on my shoulder. Though I can't say that it is really her I feel or just my wish.

The phone rings again. *Come wish beside me – don't you know you know what's right.* It is a wrong number.

Mary looks at the next picture; in it the dark girl is holding the pale woman as if she is the woman, and the woman a girl. Somewhere a bell is ringing, getting louder.

Come wish beside me – don't you know you know what's right. Mary opens her eyes. She is in her bedroom and it is flooded with light. Her mother is gently shaking her. She closes her eyes again.

The picture of the dark girl and the pale woman becomes a picture of bells: a big bell high up in a stone church; handbells rung by town criers; the bell of a mechanical clock struck by a tiny gong. Mary opens her eyes, and forgets what she has seen.

The phone rings again.

dirty boots

samuel ligon

To me, Sonic Youth's 'Dirty Boots' is about social disintegration, an existential text chronicling the various culture wars surrounding our institutions of power, government, religion, social networks, family, and conventional rock and roll itself. It's about a struggle to loose the bonds of conformity, the stultifying mores imposed on us by the commercial gods we worship, the commercial gods that make us bulimic and alcoholic, that fill us with road rage and make us slaves to Internet porn, church, heroin, television and our shitty jobs. It's about a kind of reclamation of ourselves as infinite vessels of potential, a call to heroically struggle to find our real humanity in the face of crushing oppression. Or maybe it's about fucking.

||||||||||||||||||||||||||||||||||||

The night Nikki gets caught fucking Sean in the dorm in Durham – Doug the director pounding on the door and saying her name, demanding that she open up this instant – she decides that the programme's promise of a happy future isn't worth the constant monitoring, the idiotic puritanism. That the programme's promise is worth precisely nothing. She'll never become who they want her to be, or worse, she thinks, she'll become one of them, half dead and full of fear. Sean practically cowers as he pulls his T-shirt over his head, scrambling around her bed looking for his boxers and shorts. 'Nikki,' he hisses, 'come on. Get up. Do something.' But she doesn't want to do anything, not even fuck him any more.

'Nikki,' Doug calls from the hallway. 'This is a serious violation. Open the door.' He rattles the knob. 'Or I will.'

She's not going to talk to Doug any more – Granola Doug, she calls him – not going to answer his questions or beg his forgiveness. But poor Sean is about to cry, may even be crying. 'Go out the window,' Nikki says, and Doug, slapping the door, says, 'I can't hear you, Nikki,' and Sean says, 'How am I supposed to do that?'

'Hang by your fingertips,' Nikki says. 'Then drop.'

'And break my neck?' Sean says.

'Right now,' Doug says, and Sean says, 'Get up, Nikki. Come on. Get dressed.'

Nikki's not going to get dressed. If they insist on barging into her room uninvited with a pass key, they can face her naked.

'Five seconds,' Doug says. 'I'm counting down.'

'Please,' Sean says.

'Five,' Doug says.

Sean sits on Karen's bed across the narrow room, still watching Nikki, but not pleading with his eyes any more, apparently resigned to his punishment, which he must view as catastrophic: expulsion from the programme, meaning no more monthly counselling sessions at his high school during the year, but no more summer programme at the university either, and worse, no more help clawing his way to college, the only reason any of them are here, the promise of escape, which Nikki now sees as bait for another, bigger trap, creating hope to kill it.

'Four,' Doug says.

Most of them won't finish the programme at all. Only eight students remain in this year's bridge class, the seniors enrolled in college for fall, while all the ones who've fallen away, who've come and gone the last four years, are already working versions of the shit jobs they'll have the rest of their lives. She's been stupid to believe she could make it through this and go off to college in two years, stupid to believe she could change the future.

'Three,' Doug says.

Stupid to believe anything. She can't wait two years to get away from Manchester, two years of her mother watching TV in a man's sleeveless T-shirt or dressed up and out all night, not working though she could – pretending Nikki can save them both, saying last weekend, 'I know you're smart enough, Nikki, if you can keep from fucking up. Then maybe we can get out of this shithole and I can start getting better,' spending all her nights drunk, all her days dying, poisoned by whatever lingers of the cancer that didn't kill her, or the treatment, or maybe just an idea she can't get over three years after the sickness Nikki had hoped so hard would spare her. But Nikki was just a child then, capable of believing anything: that people could get better, for instance, once they went bad, the reason Upward Bound can't change her – because she's already been changed.

'Two,' Doug says. 'You better get moving.'

Nikki looks at Sean, holding his face in his hands and staring at his shoes. Why would he want to be part of something that promises a future and then yanks it away for fucking? It doesn't make sense that two people rubbing against each other could ruin a chance for college hundreds of days away. But there Sean sits, mourning his lost future, unaware he's been Granola Doug's hostage the last three years, believing he's lost his chance when he never had one. It's not just that his mother's poor and nobody in his family has been to college. The offer of help, or his blind embrace of the offer, is what has really destroyed him.

'One,' Doug says.

Sean doesn't know that, though. Might never know it. He believes in magic. Is willing to be saved. And maybe his belief in transformation, escaping who he was born to become, will make it true. Just by believing.

Nikki watches his head jerk to the sound of the key in the lock. Poor Sean. And she's got nothing against him. Except his weakness, which isn't really his fault.

'Wait,' she calls to Doug. 'I'm getting dressed.'

'No,' Doug says, turning the knob, and Nikki screams, 'I am!' And the knob turns back and Doug says, 'You have sixty seconds,' and Nikki looks at Sean still watching the doorknob, his life draining out of him on to the tile floor.

Two weeks ago – two days ago? two hours ago? – she would have felt the same terror, at least a flicker of the doom Sean now feels, the promised future turning to ashes. She was stupid to let herself be sold on their dream, stupid to forget that hope is what kills you. When she got caught smoking the first week of this summer's session – and that seems so long ago, though it was only last month

– Nikki sat in Granola Doug's office, looking at photographs of diseased lungs, her pack of cigarettes on Doug's desk, and she promised – because they were always making you promise here, to love yourself, to believe in yourself, to be the difference, to make every situation positive – she promised as she broke the cigarettes, one by one into Doug's trash can, that she would not smoke again, at least not here on Upward Bound's time. And she kept that promise for several weeks, until she made a new promise, this one to herself, when she bought a pack of cigarettes in Manchester, home for the weekend, her mother gone God knew where, that she would never be caught again, a promise she has now broken.

'Come on,' Sean says, standing and offering his hand. 'Get dressed now.'

The only reason they did it here after hours instead of someplace outside earlier was because it was raining all day and they were so close to the end of their time together, and Karen, Nikki's poor, fat room-mate, was home with her prodigal father in Somersworth. And mainly because they wanted to. Because they felt like it. She has no idea how they got caught, if someone heard them or spotted Sean on the wrong floor twenty minutes ago. People get caught and punished here all the time, so it hardly matters how or why.

'Forty seconds,' Doug calls.

She takes Sean's hand and pulls him down to the bed.

'Nikki,' he says, and she says, 'Let's make them wait.'

'My mom's gonna kill me.'

'Let's block the door.'

'With what?' Sean says. He pulls himself from her bed and stands on Karen's side of the room, looking at Nikki, looking at the door, looking at Karen's bed, which, like the dressers and desks, is attached to the floor, everything here attached to the floor so the Upward Bounders can't walk away with anything. They only have their bodies to keep the fuckers out with, plus two chairs, some clothes and books, and Nikki's duffel bag. But she knows Doug won't force the door if they push themselves against it, that he won't risk hurting his precious charity cases or his image of himself as saviour.

'Thirty seconds,' Doug says.

Nikki stands from her bed, watching Sean watch her body, the body she's made available to him these last few weeks, pretending their first time she was a virgin because he was and it was important to him. And they've fucked and kissed and held each other every chance they've got, which hasn't been so often, not often enough, Sean believing, she knows, they're at the beginning of something, Nikki wondering whether they're at the end, another reason for taking the chance tonight, because Sean lives all the way up in Berlin at the top of the state, hours and hours and worlds from Manchester, and because he still believes in a safe kind of escape, an entrance into the white-shoe world, where he must believe they're saving a space for him, but that's what she likes about him, too, how he still believes, and Doug says, 'Twenty seconds,' and Nikki shouts, 'Will you just give me a fucking minute here, Doug! I can't find my fucking panties, OK?'

'I am giving you a minute,' Doug says.

She looks at Sean, who looks away. He just needs to be convinced.

'Now fifteen seconds.'

She knows there are staff members in the hall with Doug, plus all the students on her floor, getting off on this little drama. There are only two here she'll miss, three counting Sean: Barbara, the residential supervisor, who took her to her own house in Portsmouth two weekends ago when Nikki's mom was in jail, and Jasmine, this wicked funny chick from Dover, a junior like Sean who Nikki got baked with a couple times. They laughed and laughed, wandering the campus, the little town, pretending they were part of it. And even though he's too young, will never be as old as Nikki, and weak, she still feels tenderness for Sean, who just needs to be led.

'Is Barbara out there?' Nikki calls, and after a second in which Nikki imagines Barbara looking at Doug for silent approval to speak, Barbara says, 'I'm here, Nikki.'

'Can't we just have five minutes so I can get dressed?' she says. 'Can't I just have that tiny dignity,' *dignity* being their favourite word, along with *trust* and *commitment* and *community*, words thrown around so carelessly they mean less than nothing.

She hears murmuring on the other side of the door, then Barbara says, 'Two minutes, Nikki.'

'And not one second more,' Doug says.

She looks into Sean's eyes, which won't stay fixed on hers. Why not him? Why not now? If he's so desperate to be saved, why shouldn't she save him? They can save each other. They'll hitchhike somewhere, get jobs. 'Let's go,' she says, leading him to the window. They're only on the third floor, two flights from the ground and a row of bushes against the brick building to break their fall. But down in the grassy courtyard of Harrison Hall, looking up at Nikki's window, stand three tutor counsellors, including Susan, the chick who busted her for smoking.

'One minute,' Doug says.

Nikki waves to the crowd below, pulls Sean back from the

noise

window. 'Wait,' she says, 'I know how,' and Sean says, 'You gotta get dressed.'

'He'll take us down to the conference room to talk,' Nikki says. 'But no way he's calling our mothers tonight. Look what happened to Casey. Or Sarah. Not even Jenn got sent home in the middle of the night.'

Sean pulls away from her, picks up her tank top from the floor, her skirt, and pushes them toward her.

'We'll wait till three o'clock, when everyone's asleep,' she says. 'Then meet in front of T-Hall and take off.'

'And go where?'

'Anywhere.'

Barbara told Nikki she was self-destructive, another one of their words here, but taking off seems the opposite of that. Isn't it more self-destructive to be all alone, stuck in Manchester with her living-dead mother?

'Take these,' Sean says, the drowning back in his eyes as he pushes her clothes against her. 'Please.'

'Thirty seconds,' Doug says.

Nikki grabs her tank top, pulls it over her head. The worst part will be in the conference room downstairs, watching Sean beg for another chance for next year, shrinking, promising – what, to never fuck again? – the moment Nikki will erase him from her memory for good, and if that means eliminating a piece of herself, it's only a tiny piece she won't miss. There's nobody in this world she can talk to. Her cousin Melanie gone to Texas. Crystal still in Manchester, but already stuck there forever. Maybe Nikki should beg like Sean, hold her breath for two years, as if anyone could, then go to college with the people they've been training her to join, the people they've been training her not to offend, the fuckers with ruby slippers who were born into it.

She pulls her skirt from Sean's hand, steps into it, closing the hooks and eyes on her hip.

She'd rather be dead.

'Fifteen seconds,' Doug says.

She takes Sean's face in her hands, kisses him hard.

'I would,' Sean whispers. 'If I could. You know I would. It just doesn't make sense. I can take the bus down to Manchester whenever we want.'

'I know,' Nikki says. 'That's exactly what we'll do.' She leads him to the door.

They'll ship her back tomorrow, one day early, if they can get hold of her mom, which they won't. More likely she'll wait here with the others, go back to Manchester Friday when she's supposed to go, Sean gone tomorrow, Sean gone tonight, Sean gone in fifteen minutes, half an hour, fifteen seconds, whenever his begging becomes unbearable.

She hears the key slide into the lock. Doug says, 'I'm coming in.' The doorknob turns, the door cracks open. Nikki throws herself against it as hard as she can, slamming the fuckers back, taking deep breaths as she plants her feet and leans against the wood, planted and pushing, Doug howling in the hall, Sean behind her doing nothing to save them, until he wraps Nikki in his arms and pulls her back, lifting her from the floor, her legs kicking. Doug crashes through the door, his hand pressed over his bleeding nose, his red face furious. 'I didn't do it,' Sean says holding Nikki in the air. And she thrashes and thrashes, clawing and kicking his horrible words, blood running over Doug's mouth and chin, dripping, as he reaches for her, Sean yelling, 'She didn't mean it.'

'I did mean it,' Nikki snarls, 'you goddam pathetic fucker,' and she thrashes and thrashes, clawing and kicking, Doug and Sean grunting as she thrashes and kicks.

my friend goo

shelley jackson

I like goo. You don't know quite what it is – a pile or a puddle, an oops or anointment, repulsive or seductive. It stretches, like desire. It's sticky, like memory. It doesn't make a point, it makes a mess, P-U. So if language has a gooey side, it's when meaning makes room for the mouth. There's goo in literature, but there's even more in tongue-twisters, nursery rhymes, song lyrics. 'I know a secret or two about goo,' sings Kim Gordon, who does. Sonic Youth does to songs what I want to do to stories: pulls back the plot, ups the gurgle and squawk. 'My Friend Goo' is a song by a girl about a girl. I put the girl on a polder in an ocean of goo and let her talk.

1 ||||||||||||||||||||||||||||||||||||

The goo wheezed and flopped against the dyke. It was no-coloured, marrow-coloured, with the look of something private, something that belonged inside something else.

It was wrinkled as a scrotum, and yes, Amaranth, I do know what a scrotum looks like. (It wasn't Dad's fault, I got worried about leaving him alone so long and walked in on him.) Its swells were dry and tacky, covered with fine hair and insects, but where it broke against the dyke, it was gluey, gooey. It spindled up, then collapsed back on itself till the tip touched, forming arches that thinned to threads and snapped. It slung a cord up at a gull and yanked it back, burped up feathers like foam. During storms, it coughed hunks the size of hogs over the dyke to splat violently on the street. The puddles they made didn't stay flat – the edges crept in, the centre humped. In the dark, they looked like crouching figures. If one of them ever stood up and walked to the door of a house backed against the dyke, knocked and was admitted, nobody had ever told me about it. But I had always wondered who my mother was.

There are no pictures of my mother and my father has never spoken about her, except in a few strange and incomplete phrases, long ago: 'A book in Braille' (as you know, my father is not blind), 'A doorknob turning', 'What dogs hear' and, even more inscrutable, 'Holes in', 'When floorboards', 'You twist it' and 'Once'.

Mother may be the wrong word for what she was. I do not know that I was ever born. Maybe I came about another way. Many different objects are delivered to this shore. But I know that by the time I was aware that, instead of not existing, I existed, my 'Holes in', my 'Once', was gone.

Missing a mother did not strike me as strange. Everyone missed something. The goo had taken away the streets where our older residents had strolled, sold things and slaughtered one another. It had taken their scrapbooks, their loofahs, their names rendered in colourful animals and flowers by street artists. It had taken people too, those who had not retreated behind the dykes fast enough and those who had advanced instead, in fascination or despair.

The goo gave things, too, but not the right things.

Perhaps, I was one of the wrong things.

2 ||||||||||||||||||||||||||||||||||||||

豚は豚の歌を歌う。

The pig sings the pig's song.

The goo slapped the dyke like the palm of a hand and the tassels danced on the awning above me. The customer jumped, fumbled a piece of flotsam he had been examining, steadied it, tried to catch my eye, steadied it again, this time needlessly. 'Uh – Hey—'

'She sells seashells by the seashore.'

Now he stared. 'How did—'

Do you know how many times I've heard that? Because I do, I run a souvenir stand on the seashore, if you can still call it that – some do. Obviously, I don't shell many sea cells, she many see, see many she, sell many seashells these days, but people have taken to calling by the same name any object plucked from the goo by 'anon. beachcomber' (i.e. me) and these are what I shell – *purvey* – at my stall here on the dyke, high above the peaked roofs of our town.

The goo jumped again and the customer, looking aghast, hurried away. 'P.U.,' I whispered, adjusting the object he had disturbed. 'P.U.'

This one looked like a doll's head, its features rubbed away, merged with something the shape of an egg cup. It was the exact colour of my hand and together they made another object. I held it a moment and pretended we were fused, but when I opened my hand, we came apart easily, so I knew I still had to go home.

Home was almost invisible – chimney pots and satellite discs adrift in the fog, like a becalmed regatta of boy totes, toe boits, toy boats. Curving around them was the great dyke, visible for only a short stretch, but its coordinates pricked out by those darker objects that stuck up from the roofs below. The dyke was chalk-white concrete cast in vertical slabs. The slabs' proportions, and the seams between them, made them look like a row of teeth. Sometimes the goo, when it reared up above them, resembled a tongue. Sometimes, when it hissed and mumbled, it sounded like words, though not ones that could be found in any dictionary. This is the first language I imitated, when I began to speak. Even now, if you've noticed, I sometimes sound more like a storm than a person. When I'm self-conscious, my tongue seems to thicken or flatten into something like a rudder or an oar, unfit for the fancywork of words. I wuh-wuh-wuh-wu-wuh-*wuther*, like wind rubbing itself, goo on goo.

Since I was little, my father had given me tongue-twisters to practise on. I'm your go-to girl if 'The sixth sheik's sixth sheep's sick' needs saying. But wuthering was never the real problem. Have you ever been so ashamed that you could hardly stand to have a face and when you thought of what you'd done you had to go, 'Whatever!' or 'P.U.'? That's how I felt every time I said, 'The capital of the United Netherlands is Kansas City,' or 'That'll be seven hundred thousand dollars,' or 'Thank you, come again.' I was stupefied by the stupidity of my stupid, stupid voice saying such stupid, pointless, normal things. '*Thank you*'? Those aren't even words to me. They're – I don't know – second-hand bowling trophies – faded plastic Santas – adult diapers. Whatever! P.U.!

Maybe my father is still trying to get me to talk like a normal person when he screams, 'Good blood, bad blood! Good blood, bad blood!' Maybe he doesn't mean that I'm my mother's daughter and always will be. But I even look like the goo. My hair and eyelashes are the same no-colour as my skin. Boys call me Blondie, but I'm not, just colourless. Beige, if you like, though under this green awning, I'm practically chartreuse.

If I am my mother's daughter, and my mother is missing, does that mean I am missing, too?

If I am my mother's daughter, and I am not missing, does that mean my mother is not missing either?

And, as my father would say, if this mother-missing miss's mother isn't missing, where's the mother this miss misses?

3 ||||||||||||||||||||||||||||||||||||

Сів шпак на шпаківню, заспівав шпак півню:
„Ти не вмієш так, як я, – так, як ти, не вмію я!"
A starling sat on the starling-house and sang to the rooster:
'You cannot sing like I do, I cannot sing like you do!'

The goo takes care of me now, chucking up objects for me to sell. I have the best stock for miles and the customers know it. I never have to haggle, which is good, because P.U., I c-c-c-*couldn't*, and then how would I take care of Dad?

My father is losing a dimension. Every day, he is more like a photograph of himself and he has not said anything in years. Except for the tongue-twisters: those he's never tired of repeating – training me, I used to think, so I'd be able to speak for him when he beat his final retreat into silence. Later I figured out (imagined, you said, but you came around) that he used them to communicate – that 'A bit of better butter' could mean 'Please prepare my dinner', that 'A flea and a fly in a flue' could mean 'We are trapped, my dear. Oh, help me find the way out!' Sometimes I only understood his meaning when I repeated his words quickly several times, since it lay hidden in the slips, where the batter became bitter and the fly flew.

I got out my notebook from the chest under the table and wrote: '<u>boit</u>.'

The most important discoveries are the ones you make by accident while trying to do something else. 'Our Friend Goo': that's the title of a piece of investigative journalism I didn't write in seventh grade, since my interviews had yielded nearly nothing. I only got one answer to the question 'Where did goo come from?' and that was from my father: 'The sea ceaseth and it thuffiseff uth, sufficeth us.' People wouldn't talk about the goo, though they were nuzzled right up against it. If it made them so uncomfortable, why didn't they build out in the middle of the polders? Mr Haas (remember his toupee?) said it was convenient, using the steep back side of the dyke as a ready-made wall, but was it convenient how the rain and wind seeped through the cracks all winter? In my room at the back of the house, there were always gaps where the one curved wall met the two squared-off walls and the ceiling, and even if we grouted, the gaps opened again when the weather changed, because the dyke swelled and shrank with the seasons, like breathing. When I went into my closet and leaned against the back wall, behind the coats, I could hear it creak, and behind the creak, a quieter sound that I knew was the goo talking to itself. Or to someone else.

I did this often.

To tell the truth, very often.

Every day.

Reference books were no more helpful than my neighbours. They hardly mentioned goo at all. 'A viscous or sticky substance,' said the OED, which was obvious, and '*Fig.* sickly sentiment', which was wrong. Sometimes in fiction an author seemed to be trying to describe it, but only under the guise of a person or a landscape. My best source turned out to be children's books, and one in particular, in which a garrulous fox led a reluctant hairy biped through a series of situations that, described aloud, proved difficult to pronounce. Beside a dark blue pond, its surface ropy and peaked, where a sort of bird chewed on a taffy-like length of goo, the biped was offered some goo to chew. That author, Seuss, had written other books about goo – green goo that dripped from the sky, pink goo that ringed bathtubs and was difficult to get rid of – but what really impressed me was the association of goo with tongue-twisters.

Recently I had consulted the OED again and seen that I had missed something. Goo had a secondary meaning. 'Make an inarticulate cooing or gurgling sound like that made by a baby; converse affectionately.'

'You do look like a verb,' I told the heaving waves. But the goo wasn't talking.

4 ||||||||||||||||||||||||||||||||

Roukhi we roukhik ya roukhi roukhain be roukh matrakh ma
troukh roukhik roukhi bet roukh.
**My soul and your soul are one soul. Wherever your soul goes,
my soul also goes.**

The fog was ruining business. I decided to close up shop. I rubber-
banded the bills, stuck them and my notebook in my pocket. The
change could stay in the cash box, which went in the bottom of the
chest with the seashells. I struck the tent and stowed it in the chest,
locked the chest to the table and both to a loop of reinforcing rod
exposed at the crumbling edge of the dyke. Down the piss-stained
concrete steps into the fog.

On the way I stopped to see you, Amaranth, because you are
sometimes the only thing that thuffiseff me. You came out on your
low balcony, hiccuping amicably, and hoisted me up.

'Mr Fox, sir, I won't do it,' I said. 'I can't say it. I won't chew it.'

'Wha-*hic*?'

'Say it, chew it – as if they were the same thing. The tongue-
twister is, like, *stuff*.'

'What stu-*hic*-uff?'

'Goo. You have to chew it.' You were steering me backwards into
your room. 'Like the Goo-Goose,' I added, as you pushed me on to
your bed.

'So chew it,' you said, and put your tongue in my mouth. 'Goo-
Goose,' you said fondly, after a while. 'What do you know? My
hiccups are gone.'

Something was digging into my kidneys. I rearranged myself and a gust of warm air wafted up out of my collar. I was starting to smell like the goo, faintly cheesy. Or maybe that was Amaranth. I smashed my nose into her neck, your neck. 'You smell like me,' I discovered. 'Did you catch *Slime with Worms* this morning? I had to work.'

'No, I was at school,' you said, rather haughtily. You considered seashell-selling a dead-end job. 'Theo was asking about you again.'

'P.U.'

'So was Peter. You're very popular for someone who's never there.'

'That's my whole secret,' I said. 'Amaranth? You're not jealous of *boys*.'

'Not of boys.'

'Are you jealous of my handsome new awning?'

'Not that.'

'Are you jealous of helicopters? Tofurkeys? A hoisting or hauling apparatus consisting of a horizontal drum or axle around which a rope, cable or chain passes, turned by a crank or motor?'

'Where did you get that?'

'Are you jealous of the *Oxford English Dictionary, Shorter Edition*?'

'Not of the OED.'

'Are you jealous of this?' I pulled out the doll's head-egg cup and laid it carefully on your chest.

You frowned at it, your chin crumpling, and poked a finger into the egg cup. 'Hmm. Yes,' you said. 'I think maybe I *am* jealous of this.'

'It's for you,' I said, though I had meant to keep it.

'You're sweet,' you said, but you didn't smile. 'It's a really good one. But you keep it. It's more your kind of thing than my – *hic!*'

'Your hiccups are b-b-b-b-back,' I said.

'Now you're offended.'

I didn't disagree. I would forgive you later when you came by to apologise. I was looking forward to it.

5 ||||||||||||||||||||||||||||||||

Wie niets weet en weet dat hij niets weet weet veel meer dan
iemand die niets weet en niet weet dat hij niets weet.
**The one who doesn't know anything and knows that he doesn't
know anything knows a lot more than the one who doesn't know
anything and doesn't know that he doesn't know anything.**

When I got in, my father slowly straightened from examining a fossil oyster he kept on the sideboard, a relic from when there were oceans. 'Don Dodd's dad's dog's dead,' he informed me, several times.

'Dong Dog's deads dogs deg,' I agreed, sadly, and went to my writing desk to tally the day's take. He turned sideways to let me past, and nearly disappeared. '$150,000,' I wrote. '<u>Deg</u>.' Then I locked up the cash, took the accounts book, went to my room and closed myself in the closet.

When you're in a safe place, your face disappears, I think. There's nothing between you and what you're looking at and, if there are old coats brushing your forehead and nothing to see but darkness, all the better. After a while I pulled the seashell out of my sleeve and put it to my ear. I always try this, even though I know it's stupid. 'Mom,' I said, 'Boit deg shleets den buttle swun…'

Amaranth, if you ever need to talk to someone who isn't there, about something you don't understand, in a language you don't know, you could do worse than go to my father. You probably already realise that you'll find the words only by accident, while trying to say something else. Try 'rubber baby buggy bumper'. Dad knows hundreds and that's not even including foreign languages.

Every new word I hit upon, such as 'bubby' or 'rugger', I wrote down phonetically. I used symbols I made up myself, concentric circles, crescent moons, zigzags and little wizard hats. They were easier to remember than the ones in the dictionary and more accurate, since a few of the sounds I made were not featured in the English language. I pored over these words, trying to fit them together. Sometimes I thought I felt a gladdening inside me, telling me that I'd got something right, a word or phrase, and those I memorised. I didn't know what they meant, of course, but I had a feeling that in this case, not knowing wouldn't hurt. It might even help.

I heard something fluttering outside the door.

'Go away, Dad!'

'I wish I were what I was when I wished I were what I am,' he said.

'You're a fig plucker,' I said, rudely.

'I thought a thought,' he said agitatedly, 'but the thought I thought wasn't the thought I thought I thought.'

'Go aw-w-w-*way*!'

'White eraser? Right away, sir.'

I tried to start over, but I couldn't find the words. Finally I groped in one of Dad's ancient wellingtons for the flashlight I keep to check for spiders, mostly. Sometimes to read by. I opened my accounts book. Swun? Goist? Buttle? Sissle? Dag?

Mom?

She wasn't there.

6 ||||||||||||||||||||||||||||||||

Fekete bikapata kopog a patika pepita kövezetén
A black bull's hoof knocks on the pharmacy's chequered pavement

When I came out, Dad was watching the TV. I turned it on for him and went outside to check for you. The December fog was suffocatingly warm and thick. If I was a kid still I would have checked the sky for Santa's 'copter on its Xmas hop, sprinkling 'snow' and dropping stockings on their little parachutes. There was sometimes something good in them – candy teeth, a cat whistle – but mostly I loved the way the little red socks looked, drifting down through the fog under their white chutes. Some of them always wafted over the goo, where a wave would reach up and draw them in.

I went back inside. *Slime with Worms* was on. It was always on. In fact, it was all that was ever on, playing continuously on Channel 63, which was the only channel anyone got. *Slime with Worms* was just the name kids had given it. We couldn't tell what its real name was, if it had a name. The reception was too bad, unless it was good. Maybe the show really did take place in a dense fog and in near-total silence. Everyone complained about it, but secretly I liked the fog, the indistinct figures, the humming that rose and fell in tides, and often found myself there in dreams from which I awoke also humming.

Nobody could agree on whether it was a science programme or a how-to show or some unfamiliar kind of pornography. The figures were always touching objects to other objects with strange intensity. Then the camera would swing close to the objects, which moved furtively against one another for a while. Then something would happen. Nothing more definite than a hoof knocking against a cobblestone or a little coat being draped over a rail. You could rarely identify the objects involved, but one time I had made out what appeared to be the jawbone of a small, sharp-featured mammal (maybe a fox), being inserted carefully into an oversized padlock. Some months later, a seashell tumbled out of a wave at my feet which, if you accounted for months of being softened and mauled by the goo, could have been that very object, though the padlock was no longer iron, but the same substance as the jawbone, which itself was no longer bone, but the same firm but pliable, beigey, slightly translucent substance of which all seashells were made. I smuggled it home in my sweatshirt. It was the only evidence I had to support my private conviction that the show was broadcast by the goo, and that therefore there was a chance, however slim, that one day among the blurry figures that came and went would be my mother. I'd recognise her and call Dad, and he'd recognise her and right away he'd start thickening up, and she'd look up, just as if she could see us through the screen. Yeah, right, and then she'd come for me, over the goo, standing on a clamshell with her hair whipping around, etc.

That particular fantasy had died. But a few times over the years the same thing happened – an object I had glimpsed months before washed up on the shore. I could never be quite sure it was the same object. The picture was so blurry and the seashells were blurry in a different way, changed and softened and grown together like old memories. Still. I always took them home, thinking someday I would know what they were for.

This was one thing I had in common with other kids my age: we all loved *Slime with Worms*. It was sort of a joke, because there was nothing definite to love. The faces were blobs, when you saw them at all, so you couldn't tell the characters apart, except for 'Moustache Guy' who had a big swatch of shadow on his blob, 'Hat', whose blob had outriggers, and 'Anteater', whose blob was situated lower than the others and seemed to possess a long snout. And yet we were attached to them. Most people liked Hat or Moustache, but I liked Anteater, though there were those who said he was just a vacuum cleaner or some sort of power tool. I had even made myself an Anteater T-shirt.

Today, Moustache Guy was touching a sort of trowel to what looked like the end of a coiled rope held by Hat. Anteater appeared to be smelling the rope, or maybe his nozzle was emitting some kind of glue, you just didn't know with Anteater.

I got up and looked out the door. 'Od poklopu ku poklopu kyklop kouli koulĺ,' said Dad. It was Czech for 'The cyclops rolls the ball from one trapdoor to another'.

I closed the door. 'I have no idea what you're talking about,' I said bitterly. 'I'm going to my closet again and this time I don't want anyone to bother me. A noisy noise annoys an oyster, get it? Got it? Good.'

7 ||||||||||||||||||||||||||||||||||

Far, Fâr fâr fâr? Nej, inte fâr fâr fâr, fâr fâr lamm.

Father, do sheep have sheep? No, sheep don't have sheep, sheep have lambs.

Answers Dad has given to the question, 'Why did my mother leave us?'

'Girl gargoyle, guy gargoyle.'

'Imagine an imaginary menagerie manager imagining managing an imaginary menagerie.'

'If a white chalk chalks on a black blackboard, will a black chalk chalk on a white blackboard?'

'I saw Esau kissing Kate. The fact is we all three saw. I saw him and he saw me and she saw I saw Esau.'

'Láttam szőrös hörcsögöt. Éppen szörpöt szörcsögött. Ha a hörcsög szörpöt szörcsög rátörnek a hörcsög görcsk.'

(That's Hungarian for 'I saw a bearded hamster. It was lapping syrup. If a hamster is lapping syrup, it will be seized with a hamster-clamp'.)

8 ||||||||||||||||||||||||||||||||||

Maziņš eža puskažociņš uz šaursliežu dzelzsceļa.

A little half-length, hedgehog fur coat on a narrow-gauge railroad track.

'Dead,' I whispered. 'I mean, deg.'

After a while the golden L outlining the bottom and side of the door began to lighten the darkness. I couldn't see, but when I moved my eyes I got the feeling of shapes.

The first time I misspoke one of my new words, I was confounded. Was it even truer, more perfect now? But sometimes – often – twisting a twisted word just untwisted it. For blug, bug or blood. For deg, dead. Maybe the speech I thought was normal, whatever, P.U., was just twisted so far it had come back around. Maybe when I thought I was making sense, I wasn't. Or if I was, it was insignificant compared to the crucial nonsense I was making simultaneously and by the very same means.

In the back of the closet was the faintest possible gleam. It could have been in the back of my eyes instead. Was it the wing of a beetle, the head of a nail? I moved my head to the left and it vanished. Back, it reappeared. I turned on my flashlight. Rust-rouged concrete wall jumped forward. In the brightness the gleam was lost. I turned off the flashlight, waited for my eyes to lose their memory of the wall. The gleam returned. I fixed my eyes on it and turned on the flashlight.

A dot.

A drop.

A blob.

It was growing?

I put my finger on the blob. It felt like nothing – like the wall. I looked at the smear on my finger. It was no colour, with the look of something that belonged inside something else.

When I was little, I thought a lot about the insides of things. A closet, a nutshell, a big red rubber ball: opening them only told you what was in an *open* closet, busted ball or shell. Even if you did somehow know what was in there, you couldn't talk about it. The nut still in the shell – the not-yet nut – the almond before it was white: describing it was like cracking the shell. The minute you named it, that wasn't what it was, even if – this is the tricky bit – it maybe had been, the moment before. You could name it only without knowing you had named it, and probably with a word no one had ever used before, a word you could use without lying, because you had no idea what it meant. A word like—

I scooped up a bit of the goo on the tip of my finger, where it reformed itself into a nearly spherical blob – a gubby, a dod, dag – deg.

If 'deg' sounded right, was it really because it was a word in a secret language? Or precisely because it was nonsense?

'What is the point of talking nonsense?' you had asked me once.

'Maybe that's what the fox meant by 'chew it',' I'd answered.

But maybe he meant, chew it.

I chewed it.

It was a bit like chewing on my own tongue. It tasted like I tasted, tasting it, like the taste of taste itself, before it had anything specific to taste. But imagine you had never tasted that before.

Like someone else with my birthday.

The way a lost scarf looks when you go back for it.

The stain on the headband of a baseball cap.

When you can't tell where the smell is coming from.

A book in Braille (I can't read Braille).

A little half-length hedgehog fur coat on a narrow-gauge railroad track.

|||||||||||||||||||||||||||||||||||

Драбина з повиламуваними щаблями
A ladder with broken steps

When I came out, you were sitting on my bed. What a relief, I hated you. I stalked past you into the bathroom and used a hand mirror to shine the light down my throat, which felt unusual. I saw something no-coloured shining and flexing way back down, like a second, deeper tongue. The better to eat you with. Could it taste? When I found out, I whispered, '*Roukhi we roukhik ya roukhi roukhain be roukh matrakh ma troukh roukhik roukhi bet roukh.*' I didn't tell you what it meant, I thought you'd know.

But somehow, that was when things started to get the way they got between us, how you didn't want to hear about the shells any more, what I was building with them, and how I started hiding them from you and you went on that date with Theo and I followed you and you confronted me and all I could say was 'an enemy amenome an anomie a menome anemone' and Theo went home and I went home and it turned out that Dad was caught in an eddy and had been blowing around and around and around in circles all evening and that night I ate a whole bucket of goo and shat my pyjamas in my sleep, sort of shat, I mean it was translucent, it was shining, I never told you. My tradegy strategy, tragedy stragity, tragedy strategy.

I wrote about all that but I erased most of it. Maybe I see my father's point of view: some things should be hard to say. Here's all that's left:

Als jouw tekkel mijn tekkel tackelt, tackelt mijn tekkel jouw tekkel terug.

If your dachshund tackles my dachshund, my dachshund will tackle your dachshund.

Als een potvis in een pispot pist, heb je een pispot vol potvispis.

When a whale pisses in a pisspot, you get a pisspot full of whale piss.

Egy kupac kopasz kukac, meg még egy kupac kopasz kukac, az két kupac kopasz kukac.

One heap of bald maggots plus another heap of bald maggots makes two heaps of bald maggots.

Kuku kaki kakak kakekku kaku.

My great-uncle's toenails are rigid.

10 |||||||||||||||||||||||||||||||||||

O tempo perguntou pro tempo quanto tempo o tempo tem, o tempo respondeu pro tempo que o tempo tem tanto tempo quanto o tempo que o tempo tem.

The time asked the time how much time the time has, the time answered the time that the time has as much time as the time that the time has.

It was not a very big hole, so it was not a very fast leak, but the hole got bigger, the leak got faster.

Some more objects I thought I recognised washed up: a decoy duck with a smooth knob for a head, a gear twisted into an 8, a boomerang with a pouch. I added them to the pile in my room. It struck me that they were like the new words I was trying to learn: familiar and strange at the same time. Maybe they made sentences. *Slime With Worms*: it was a show about fitting things together. That was so obvious, I had missed it! I tried pushing the decoy duck knob into the egg cup and it snapped right in, dutter mudded dop. The 8 gear fit on the boomerang grip. I was building something, I just didn't know what it was yet.

Every day I went into the closet and closed the door and stood there leaning against the plastic shrouding my father's old suits, the hair on my arms standing up, and even though the goo was for a long time not much more than a puddle, I could feel it coming up around me, and when it had risen to my knees I already felt it licking my stomach, and before long it seemed to me that I was in it right up to my neck, and eventually I was.

You came by the house a few times. 'I looked for you up on the dyke,' you said, 'but I didn't see your stall.'

'I'm not selling the seashells any more,' I said. Neither of us looked at the thing on the floor.

'So how are you?'

'I'm fine,' I said. 'K-k-k-k-k-keeping busy.' *P.U., P.U., P.U., P.U., P.U.*

When you left, I went back in the closet.

It's complicated, mourning for someone who's gone and at the same time isn't, like my father, like my mother, and now I'm passing that on to you. I realised that the day I felt you outside the closet, holding the doorknob and not turning it. You were right not to and I wouldn't have let you anyway – I was hanging on from the inside – but I'm sorry I didn't say anything. I couldn't, though. My mouth was busy. I tried to make my hand apologise, in the way it damped the rattle of the spindle in the latch. But I know how hard it is to understand even words.

Eventually, you went away, and that was the day I went in over my head, and when I came out again, I knew what I was building.

Amaranth, the stall is yours if you want it. You know where I keep the keys. Take anything from the house, too, but go soon. I'm not the little Dutch boy. I never even thought of plugging that hole. Eventually, the closet won't hold the goo. Then the house won't hold it. Oh, sure, a repair crew will get there in time, but there are other leaks, other kids with something hidden in their closets. One way or another, a flood is coming. My mother told me so.

I wish I could say I knew it would all be all right, that there will be time to reach high ground. But my advice is, start building a boit.

The instructions are included among these papers. But if you read without moving your lips, you won't find them.

11

Meisje met je mooie mondje moet je met je maatje mee?
Little girl with the beautiful mouth, do you have to go with your mum?

'We're going on a trip, Dad,' I said. 'See, I made a bot. Boit.' I showed him how lightly the sall glid when you fithed the buttle, and how when you edidud, the sush cleverly blad the deg, making the menamy dop just enough to let the siz fill.

'Are our oars oak?' he said. The goo clucked under the selm.

'Or zar zar zork.'

'Sure she's shipshape?'

'Surceash sipsape, sir!'

He sheeted himshelf in the farn with an interested expression.

'Toet toet te tit tat tut es.'

'Yes, yes, it is time that it is finished,' I agreed.

protect me you

eileen myles

This song reminds me of my dog who died when she was sixteen. I saw Kim [Gordon] in those final months at the end of last year and Kim told me about an animal communicator I should talk to to find out why Rosie was staying alive. I did find out. The communicator talked to Rosie and Rosie just liked the smell of life. She spoke in very special radiant terms and the communicator thought my dog was quite a poet. Last time I saw Kim she asked me if I had ever connected with the communicator. I didn't get a chance to tell her I had and it was quite a success. The song talks about being sixteen like Rosie was and I think the song has some of her need and her weird openness. Plus I just love the title. It's like a coin.

||||||||||||||||||||||||||||||||

There's something I can't see – a helicopter behind all the trees and everything. It's a lazy description but there's not much to say. All it is is sound and then it's gone. But you've just fallen down on the grass. I thought this would be a nice place to sit in the afternoon. The cat shows up, black, looking out. When I'm surrounded by trees, a condition I've sought out pretty persistently throughout my life, I think the thing I might like the most about them is this whisper like all the hair of the world passing through the tunnel of one single breath – if that is a form of percussion. This irregular hiss of trees and wind. I think it is my mother. And I am her son, and you are my dog.

Our relationship is part discomfort & humiliation and part devotion. Oh once upon a time I wanted a dog exactly as much as I wanted to be alive. Maybe I didn't even want a dog then. I wanted to say I was alive. Even to be a dog would be enough and so if I could be seen wanting one and could begin asking for it incessantly – if I could summon up asking in every possible manner. Please. Leaving notes under pillows and toilet seat covers. Did I want a dog, really? No I was a kid who was desperate to be seen in a state of desire & supplication. That was many years ago. I wanted to already be my yes. A positive child in a state of knowing & reaching out. Not for myself but towards a friend. The child was denied. In the manner of my family they said yes and then they said no. Somewhere there is a picture of this. A little boy in bangs and a plaid cotton shirt. I remember it was red but the picture was taken with my father's Polaroid land camera which only took black & white photos then which added to the beauty of them because the past is so often a place whose colours are only in my mind. How hard it would be to be a movie star. To be in full colour in front of everyone. To be applauded and owned. Isn't that like being a very good dog? You're lashing out at photographers who are adamant about capturing you, your every movement, again and again. I admit I've wanted to be a movie star to be seen in that disgraceful and hungry way – the buttered toast of everyone. There I am with my beautiful smile. A big piece of bread. Angry, covering my face. I held my dog in the black and white world and I knew that this was the moment I had wanted so keenly. To be still, to be fixed, to be sad. I was just like a little prayer card holding my dog. I would never know myself again as clearly. Did that dog go on to her death when we returned her to the ASPCA after that one long crying night that disturbed my mother to no end? A tree will push this way and that, be permanent in its breath of time. It's hardly the colour it is, a white pole, some green some red. I would think a tree would know exactly what it was and be so peaceful. As long as she's breathing a dog is not at rest. So I was a child who wanted a dog. I became myself. I certainly wasn't thinking I wanted a dog the day we met. I was watching the rollers turn. I mean time. You have to touch on something repeatedly but what could it be? How could that happen if time was your problem? What could you touch?

That's why I'm a poet. Even in the bathtub as a child I was syncopating my blubs because I didn't know what to do with the light and the wetness and my mother and when would it stop. I had a horror of life's never-endingness which made me really hate art. Its spectacles. Rodeos. Circuses. People skating around on ice. And in the world on ponds. My feet hurt. And look – all the trees have lost their leaves and are black. Isn't it time to go in? It seems like the people around me wanted to do happy things and a child is supposed to be a little dog and bark happily in response – at the ice & the trees & the day. And now here it is all around us.

This morning I was reading in the paper how the governor of

New Jersey a secret gay man had *hired* a poet of all the ludicrous persons on earth to be his director of homeland security. And then the poet realised the governor wanted him. How unabashedly corrupt of a governor to entice a total fool – a poet – practically a clown's occupation to take care of the people of a state. The state of New Jersey, at that. The governor wanted the poet to hold him and love him and kiss his toes. Possibly the governor wanted to exercise his dominance over the poet shoving his penis in the poet's butt. I had already heard parts of this story, mostly about the governor's secret gayness, but it seems like they saved this one tiny detail for the end. The fact that the young man was appointed to a position in which he could only reveal his incompetence – who could blame him for that. He was young, after all. But the later, more laughable titbit. Like the room stopped laughing and then the little dog lifts its butt and poops. Homeland security! How could a poet do that? How could a *poet* do that? Twice a fool. And twice the governor's crime.

And speaking of such – now that we've seen really good photos of how really bad it was in New Orleans and we've seen also that even the man in charge *there*, Brownie, knew about horses, not safety, there were problems really much bigger than his unknowing, the unknowing is always getting larger, and we've looked at them all publicly together, and realise that there are always people of greater authority equally incompetent, people like the president who owned a baseball team and laughed publicly at a woman, Aileen, he whinnied at her who was being sent (by him) just then to the electric chair – he mocked her.

And supposedly when he was governor, he actually improved schools that was his big claim but now we've learned that in fact the books were cooked, that's all. And the schools got even worse under him and when he was a kid he used to blow up squirrels and he farts in front of his interns today – kids who went to good schools and studied hard – I'm not particularly impressed by those leadership types living or dead, maybe if one gets shot or mugged you see the kid's picture in the paper and think – what a shame he or she got good grades. But say he survives – winds up delivering papers to the Oval Office and there's the president laughing & farting. And you tried hard & he hadn't and now he's your boss and you've got to smell his farts. You're a dog.

The final insult to everyone was that what little New Jersey had to protect itself with was a poet. There's a little red up in the trees. And my dog wants to go upstairs. And I probably should let her have her way. Because she is dying.

Not only are her legs stiff but her joints are swollen and covered with sores. I don't have another life partner. It's almost five decades after the perfect photograph of my desire and because she's pacing all over the house and slobbering her food, the ants are swarming around her like candy. She's a sweet dying clump. Today is the day when summer turns into fall. Surely the light is shorter or longer today. My planet is in some angle to the sun that people say this is September a beautiful month when it's not too hot possibly the sweetest time of the year. There are already waves and waves of what I am saying. I've set something in motion I can return to again and again. Anywhere. Dogs begin barking. You have never been a barker unless you were left outside a café tied to a post, then you yelped like hell. You like company.

I do too. I've discovered I'm an essentially social person. I like to sit in groups, or move with them. I like when they all decide to go see some art or celebrate the number of years a person's been on the planet. I even like when they all get loaded in honour of that. Though I get out of the room fast. I go for the rebounding energy of heys and hugs and awkward kisses and the opportunity to raise my flag and see it light up in your eye. Your flag tells me where I want to go next. It's like the world I live in is a field of flags whapping and waving and I want to see them all waving. I want to stand in the crowd or the small group. I like the small and large crowds that talk about how they feel. Who listen to one another, who let the collective listening and talking build up a head of swarming energy that fills and delights us. These are actually the groups that showed me that I do like groups. I like to be alone. But then I need to talk to someone. I like God. When I was a child I was taught that there was someone listening and I chanced tiny hellos that frequently felt empty but longer conversations often silences felt like I was sitting in an enormous radio, like I had big earphones on when I felt separated from the world but turned into this show. And that's where you came in. Whether you listen or not, you're in there too. My dog. You're a part of the great silent show of this morning's sun. Turns out it was the most even day of the year, one of the two when dark and light counterbalance each other. I have a round board in my house with balls underneath and I climb on while I'm waiting for water to boil or trying to escape the pressure inside, not God but a kind of weather I inhabit & control. I think it comes from Ireland which is why I feel I need to live there for a few years just to understand the minerals and substances that spawned me. I come from Poland too but I live with Poland. This is Poland. Ireland is the mystery, Ireland is gone but, like magic, it calls me home. I get on the board in my house it's in the kitchen so there's a square window. When I was a child we lived across the street from the ocean. It was a perfect spot. I learned to make sandwiches for myself in that house. That was adolescence. Squeezing a pepper and making it spurt. Eating my own food with you. In the sun. At last my life had begun. I had one job which was to do the dishes after dinner with my young arms and there was a stone church outside the window its bell. Sounds spreading out and landing in the marsh.

Up on my board I look out the window in my kitchen. That animal glance is enough. To connect me to the first suns, the first light and jobs. To be in and out within the reach of square light. The round board at first seeks to confound me. One orientation is pure reaching forward so you attempt to not tip yourself, not quite jerking back but asking a wave not to curl and you beg by little movements of your hip. Another, the side to side orientation demands that you use some bell inside your crotch to ring in the middle so to speak and there is a glorious feeling of hip no dick sway it makes me want to dance, and my calves planted and working, working continually. I discovered a new direction the other day I mean I had always been aware that the board made me TALL. It was simply that and there were people I wanted to be tall around and I mostly accomplish that with boots but you know boots aren't really for walking they're for promenading so you're going around on stilts in a way. You won't fall but when you think about them, and for all the pleasure of being a little higher the trade-off is your own absence from presence. You're losing your own fealty to the ground. Which can't be ignored. You lose your earth for your sky. When I'm on the board in my kitchen, when I get still, just for a click I am high – I think *oh...*

kissability

laird hunt

Late autumn. Late nineties. Early evening. The Pink Pony. Manhattan. Ludlow Street. A flock of kids flies past in fake leather jackets, punk pants. Eyes flashing. One of them says, 'Fuck this.' I'm standing there. Waiting? Hands in pockets. Breath coming in clouds. Car pulls up, caught mid-block behind a cab. Finger flicks ash out the window. Other hand simultaneously pushes play. 'Kissability'. Volume mounts. Heads turn. Car pulls away, turns, gets caught again. 'You've got kissability...' Vaguely muted, lovely scraping along brick, over asphalt, past parked cars. Flock of kids now coming back. Smiles on their faces. Breath steaming the air. Coming fast. All too perfect. 'You fly hard...'

well ||||||||||||||||||||||||||||||

My mother said, $15 a night, and the first one said, we'll think about it, and the second one said, we'll take it, and my mother said, that's fine. We'll just go get our bags, then, the first one said. Our bag...

we share, the second one said. But I had already dipped my hand through the open window into the cool, cracked-vinyl depths of their Pinto and was coming up the walk with their suitcase when they turned. The fuck, the first one said. Oh, hey, we'll get that, the second one said. Here it is, I said, as they came towards me, but kept my fingers hooked around the handle so that if they wanted it they would either have to effleurage my knuckles or stand there where I could get a good look at them and wait for me to let go. My goddam lucky day: they did both – hands sweeping in only to sweep back out, not quite (double effleurage) in time. I'll carry it in for five bucks or some ice cream, I said. We got it, thanks, they said. Addison, my mother said. The first one smelled like lemons. The second one like limes or grapefruit or something. Or vice versa. Whatever – there was citrus happening. I counted beads of sweat, my eyes flicking from first to second, second to first. I got to seven each before my mother fired off an 'AD-di-Son', and I let go. The second one smiled, sort of sweet, so I ignored him and smiled at the first one, who was biting the inside of his cheek and looking over my shoulder, maybe at their crap car or our crap street or crap town. This is Addison, my mother said. We're related. We all mumbled this and that and then they were in the house doing God knows what the fuck, and I was sitting in their car where the bag had sat with my shorts and shirtsleeves rolled up getting some afternoon sun.

and ||||||||||||||||||||||||||||||

I had dozed and was half-dreaming about something involving a violet teapot and a band of light that had left the sky and moved in next door because the nude sunbathing was good or something fucked up like that when the second one leaned his head in the window and said, boo. Boo yourself, I said. I sat up and felt some of the seat come up with me. It's stuck to my back isn't it, I said. Little grey-yellow flecks, he said. Grey-yellow, is that even a colour? I pulled one off my shoulder and looked at it. I wouldn't call that grey-yellow, I said. Well, that's what we call it. I'd call it ochre or quince maybe. We call it grey-yellow, it's our car. Who's we? He's taking a nap – we drove all night. Does he snore? No, but I do. Which one of you is older? We're the same age. Same birthday? We're twins. Yeah, you look a lot alike. Fraternal – same litter, different eggs. Yuck. I'm sorry. Don't be. We bantered on for a while. My mother often uses a kind of fake basso Ha, Ha, Ha with her friends on Monopoly nights. I used this Ha, Ha, Ha to solid effect with him. He had developed fresh sweat droplets and smelled like a tangerine. His jaw quivered a little when he thought about things. Or when he looked like he was thinking. Fuck knows. He gave me the upshot, the lowdown. They had come a long way and now they were going to do some business in Shitsville only he didn't call it that. He kept saying 'your town'. I told him about my town. I took out my biggest brush and painted him some thick strokes. You should drive me somewhere for an ice cream, I said. I could just murder a soft-cone.

and

The first one came up behind the second one so quietly that he had him in a wicked headlock before I knew what had happened, and I have excellent senses according to a battery of standardised tests administered at my lame school. They wrestled around all fraternal and same litter and et cetera, and I brushed off my shoulder and rolled my shorts back down and otherwise prepared myself for non-gratification *in re* the soft-cone. I was not wrong. Beat it, sugar, the first one said. Why do you guys wear those weird suits? I said. Weird? said the first one. Tailor-made, said the first one. Camel–silk blend, said the first one. We were talking about her town, the second one said. I'd like an ice cream, that's what we were talking about, I said. Wouldn't we all, said the first one. Wouldn't we all. He was, undoubtedly, the more aesthetically appealing brother. The other one had nice sweat patterns and the tangerine thing, but this one had the sweat plus lemons plus explosions in his eye sockets and beautiful hands the size of fat hardbacks. Ice cream, I said again, flashing lots of fresh, young enamel, knowing I was about to be standing in the grass watching them drive off. The car sounded about like it looked. Nice suits, I yelled after them. You look like Al Capone. Let me get my machine gun. Addison, propel your butt in here this goddam instant, my mother said.

SO ‖‖‖‖‖‖‖‖‖‖‖‖‖‖‖‖‖‖‖‖‖‖‖‖‖‖

Once my mother had finished giving me some flame-broiling about my comportment and sloppy attire and inappropriate attitude and need for a shower and some grooming, I grabbed the spare key and went up to their room. The bed under the south eaves was hot and rumpled so I reclined on it and played listening-staring-corpse-chick, listening to the wall unit pour out its cold air, listening to Mr Crocker or someone run his pukey mower, staring up at the whorls of wood and the slant of the ceiling, staring at the backs of my pretty-nice hands. By and by, I composed a poem that began,

> I lie here on your bed
> And even though I'm dead
> There's fine stuff in my head

And ended

> Once we're safely wed
> And I've traded white for red
> I will still inspire dread.

Then I got up and opened their suitcase. It was full of the usual travelling crap, like they all have, all the guys who stay here, all jumbled up. I sort of swished it around a little with my index fingers, trying to remember which way egg-beaters turned: right beater clockwise, left beater counter? Vice versa? There was a plastic bag with some shaving cream and a razor in it. There was a can of shoe polish. There was a comb with some of its teeth missing. There was a book of stories by Hemingway. There was an oversize Arkansas-is-for-Lovers belt buckle without a belt. There was a pair of Mickey Mouse flip-flops. Ha, Ha, Ha, boys, I said. After which I put on a pair of blue boxers and a wrinkled white shirt, took them off, did a headstand that I held for a twenty count, then went downstairs because I thought I heard the phone.

although ||||||||||||||||||||||||||||

It was dark and I waited, first on the front porch, then outside their door, then on the couch in the living room under the ceiling fan, then in the high grass under the fireflies, then at the kitchen table as my mother and I ate pork chops that she had burned worse than usual, then in front of the TV, then in the garage by the box of comic books, then out on the sidewalk where the mosquitoes got me, then balancing on the roof of the long-empty doghouse under the stars, then back on the couch in the living room, then on the phone although everyone was on vacation, then in the shower where I shaved and zoomed and buzzed and hummed, then up in their room, then down in my room, in the basement, where the posters stared at me and the walls creaked and some motherfucker cricket went to work.

inevitably |||||||||||||||||||||||||||||||

The kitchen heating vent and my bedroom's heating vent sit one on top of the other, which is (understatement) annoying when my mother has Monopoly night, given that she and her friends are all drinkie drinkie and double word score whatever for hours at a time. Not so annoying this time. Yeah, said the first one. You bet, said the second. Ha, Ha, Ha, said my mother. I sat up. Still black out. My clock had been blinking midnight for days. I lay back down, sound was better there, right under the vent, kind of a clear channel. A Swede? my mother said. Big guy, used to put on the gloves, had some luck, said the first one. Usually eats at the diner – every night except tonight. Didn't show tonight, said the second. Which diner? said my mother. Greasy little place, said the second. By the station, said the first. A Swede? said my mother. Like clockwork – every night until tonight. We need to see him. There are lots of big guys around – you say this one's Swedish. Some kind of Scandinavian. Northern persuasion, has a nose looks like a loaf of bread. He's all punched out. Well, I might know him to look at him and I might not. Fair enough. Why are you looking for him? Business. We need to see him. I swung my legs over the edge of the bed, pulled on my shorts and went up. The second one had his left hand in his glass fishing for an ice cube. The first one's eyes went Kabam! My mother had her hair pulled back and some ear candy on. Yeah, right – dream on, I thought. *I* know a Swede, I said.

or moonlight

Ice cream, I said. I'd shown them my Swede. That's the one, they'd said. They'd gone right over to him and sat down on either side of the bed where he was lying with the covers pulled up to his chin, breathing deeply, blue eyes carefully blinking, and they had clapped him on the shoulder and chucked his cheeks and told him he needed a shave and a shower or a bath or some cologne, and then they had discussed bogs and quicksand and concrete modalities, just, they had said, for the fuck of it, then they had clapped him on the shoulder again and had asked me to step outside and wait for them so they could do something and then take me home. Out they had come. Nice moonlight, said the first one. Lovely, said the second. Ice cream now, I said.

noise

home ||||||||||||||||||||||||||||||||

The Pinto let out a couple of sharp pops and pings that echoed off the school and smacked me on the face, making the earrings I had borrowed from my mother jangle, and the second one groan. The first one said, lead on, and I led on, Quick Stop soft-cone coating my fingers, tickling my wrists, over the glinting asphalt and on to the high grass of the football field, the cool grass, the dark grass, the you wouldn't dare grass, where the first one said, don't run, and the second one said, you won't, will you? and I said, run? A minute later the first one said, spot's as good as any other, and the second one said, good spot, so we all sat down, and I started licking my fingers, which is when the sirens started up in the distance and the first one said, oh fuck, and the sprinklers came on.

snare, girl

catherine o'flynn

This story wasn't inspired by any single track or lyric – more just the mix of emotions and sensations I experience when listening to Sonic Youth. I wanted to try and capture that nihilist, elemental, caustic flavour. I think it's good music to listen to whilst locked in the boot of a car.

||||||||||||||||||||||||||||||||

Naomi didn't know what was sticking in her back. At first, all there had been was blackness and her breath coming short and fast, but as the hours had passed she'd pieced together an intimate knowledge of her new surroundings. The metal surface pressing against the top of her head was a toolbox, the stiff fabric at her feet some kind of tarpaulin, in front of her she knew was her school bag, and under her was something softer than cheap carpet – maybe a picnic blanket. Mr Lynwood was the type of man who would have a picnic blanket in his car boot, he probably had pimply PVC runners over his carpet, and nasty arm covers on his sofa to absorb the unspeakable fluids that seeped out of his skin. She couldn't work out what was sticking in her back, though. It felt firm and rounded, like a body. Surely there wasn't another one in there with her. She tried to suppress another fit of shaking. It seemed to go in cycles – a phase of blind panic followed by a spell of calm and heightened clarity. She was trying to cling to the calm, she didn't think her heart could stand another surge of adrenalin.

She tried to imagine all that was being done to find her. Her parents would have contacted the police by now. Her dad would hate that, he fought against any suggestion that everything wasn't running exactly as he predicted. When the kitchen ceiling collapsed some months earlier, narrowly missing her mother, he said he'd long been expecting an incident of that nature. She remembered him poking the fallen masonry with his toe and nodding his head. He'd make her mother phone around before he called the police. Naomi thought back to the friends she used to have, their faces merged into one indistinct pink smudge. They'd tell her mother that they never saw her out of school any more.

She couldn't stop shaking, but couldn't tell now whether it was fear or the low temperature in the boot. It had been five hours. She didn't know where she was. She concentrated hard and tried to remember any features of the journey, but it was no good – all she knew was that they had been moving for about an hour. She could be outside Mr Lynwood's house, maybe he was inside watching TV, or maybe he'd driven somewhere else and left the car. The car had stopped, the door had opened, she had clenched every muscle in her body and then gradually exhaled as the door to the boot remained closed.

A terrible thought occurred to her. What photo were they using?

Why hadn't she thought of this before? Her mind reeled. She thought of the photos that her parents chose to display. Pitiless family shots with Naomi at the back scowling through heavily kohled eyes and an angry mask of acne. Worse still, the school photos, every one of which was displayed on the sideboard. The early ones with just-brushed static hair and tearful eyes; the mid-period gap-toothed smile; the latter phase with the face largely obscured by the long black curtain of hair. She thought of last year's. The photographer had broken wind loudly and lengthily with no comment just as he was taking her photo. Naomi's expression was captured for ever. Was that the backdrop behind the local newsreader's appeal for information? Was that the A4 flyer being shown from door to door?

Her hands and feet were tied, but she was able to move her hands together and reach into her bag. She put one earphone in and pressed Play. Lying in this dark space, listening to music wasn't so different to any other evening. At 5.15 she would fly through the door after school like a leaf blown in by the wind. She'd throw her bag in the hallway and run upstairs to her room, slamming the door behind her and placing a chair against it. She'd go straight to her record player and put the needle at the start of the album already sitting on the turntable and then collapse on to her bed – feeling that she could breathe again. The music flowing straight to her lungs. Someone would knock at her door, a voice would shout, but she was somewhere else. She'd stare at the wallpaper at the side of her head and become lost somewhere in a landscape made up of the abstract shapes in the pattern of the paper and the music.

There were many songs about love. Those were the kinds of songs that her classmates listened to and she didn't. Recently, though, she'd begun to see a certain truth to the lyrics, they captured some of what she felt – their only error was in attributing such feelings to love. What the words described to her were the manifestations of pure hatred. The power of hate. Hate at first sight. Hate changes everything. These she understood. Mr Lynwood had entered the classroom in September, he'd introduced himself and she'd felt the thunderbolt strike. It was like an allergy, a chemical reaction. His fuzzy hair, his ridiculous shoes, the bobbling on the hips of his slacks, the way he breathed. Everything about him repulsed her. She couldn't bear to look at him and yet couldn't stop thinking about him. Each morning she would wake up and her first thought would be how many times she would have to see him in the day ahead. He was slimy, he was patronising, he wanted desperately to be liked and yet none of this could adequately explain the intensity of her feelings. What she felt was hissing, claws-out, fur-and-feather, bone-deep, animal.

She imagined an alien looking down on planet Earth. Among the trees and the mountains, among the cities and the fields, among the rooftops and the streets there was a girl tied up in the boot of a car listening to the same track over and over again. But Naomi couldn't feel herself to be a speck. Instead she felt the universe contract and shrink to the size of this boot and she was at the centre of the black cosmos floating in the music. It was pure chance that she'd noticed one day that he never locked his car. Clearly he trusted 'the kids'.

If, back before Mr Lynwood joined the staff, someone had ever bothered to ask her what the worst thing about school was, she would have had difficulty in choosing. Maybe the cold sweat of anxiety each morning waiting for the bus and not knowing who was going to be on it. Maybe the pain in her shoulders from keeping them clenched all day long. Maybe the afternoons that never seemed to end. Maybe the existence of netball. Now, though, she knew that the worst thing was her inability to change a single thing. Her dad would bitch and moan about his job. He'd tell her to enjoy the freedom of her school days and she would have to fight the urge to throw a cup at him. He could decide to go in late the next day, he could decide to go to work by car or train, he could decide to take his holidays in February, he could even decide to leave his job altogether and go and work somewhere new, and he wanted sympathy from her.

Her email the previous day said simply: 'Please stop this or I'll call the police'. There was a chance he might have told a colleague, but she was sure he'd try and talk to her first. A disturbed student was such a great opportunity for him to practise his pastoral care skills. He spent his days imploring them to tell him their personal problems. Totally confidential. Maybe something they wouldn't feel comfortable talking to their parents about. The thought of it made her gag. His class was last period and he asked her to stay behind in front of everyone, just as she'd hoped. To be alone with him, to elect to spend even a few extra moments in his company, cost her a lot. It was hard to do, but she had to win the right to decide.

She couldn't understand why she didn't ache more. She'd get the odd spasm of cramp but not the kind of agony you might expect from being curled up in the boot of a Vauxhall Astra for six hours. She wondered whether adrenalin was a painkiller. She was aiming for eight hours. After that time she'd try and attract a passer-by with banging and shouting. It was tricky not knowing exactly where the car was parked, or how nearby he was – she had to ensure that the passer-by would hear her, but he would not. Her sole aim, the one decision she was forcibly making, was simply never to see him again. She didn't care whether he went to prison or not as long as he never returned to her school and she never had to think of him again.

When the rest of the class had left the room and he was about to speak she said that she needed to go to the toilet urgently. She walked out to the car park, pressed the button and climbed into his boot. Before she'd tied the rope around her feet and hands she placed a few images she'd downloaded from the Internet around the boot. There were others on the CD they'd find in his briefcase. They were unnecessary really, a missing girl in the boot is all it would take.

She started the track again. The guitar scoured her and made her flesh feel raw inside and out. Thurston screamed he was inhuman, but it wasn't quite working. She couldn't lose herself in the noise, she was still aware of place and time. These final hours would not pass. She was aware of her body, but instead of the pain she'd expected, she felt a kind of swelling, lurching nausea. She was lying on Mr Lynwood's rug, inhaling the hamstery smell of his boot, and she wondered whether she could ever scrub herself clean. She pulled the earphone out and all she heard was the blood beating in her ears.

She rehearsed the next stage in her head. Her rescue from the boot, the look on her parents' faces, the absence of Mr Lynwood from school the next day and the days after that. She supposed the police would question her, but she had her story straight. Her parents would want her to talk too. She thought of the questions they would ask, and she realised that she would be forced to think about Mr Lynwood when answering them. She wondered how long they'd insist it was necessary to discuss it. After that he'd be deleted from her head for good. Unless it went to court, but she'd refuse that. She couldn't have done all this and still have to see his face ever again. She tried to focus on a future without his shadow cast over it. She imagined walking the school corridors and never hearing his fake laugh, never seeing his fatuous, clumsily written comments on her homework, never feeling his eyes upon her. But, though Mr Lynwood would be gone, her name and his would be on everybody's lips, her name and his joined for ever in classroom mythology. With sudden clarity she realised there was no end to him. She started to shake again, but this time more violently. She struggled with the rope and untied her hands and feet. She felt his presence all around her, in the blanket, in the tools, in the tarpaulin, and it felt like an appalling intimacy. She imagined him putting his groceries into this boot, his toothpaste and toilet paper and tinned soup all around her, and these glimpses of his life were too much to bear. She felt the bile rising in her throat as she started hammering on the boot and screaming.

Later, as she ran from the startled woman who found her, the stars shone above in the clear night sky, the dark streets opened up ahead of her and the black space she'd burst from propelled her forwards into the ever expanding universe and the inescapable cloud of her own breath.

brother james

emily maguire

When I was fourteen I was in love with chaos, and that's what I thought I heard in Sonic Youth's music. Manic, panicked and seemingly deliberately senseless, it was like the inside of my brain amplified. I would listen through headphones, volume on full, until I was nauseated. Repeated listening, however, revealed structure and intention beneath the sound and fury. The power of purposeful frenzy, directed rage and calculatedly unhinged passion was a revelation.

||||||||||||||||||||||||||||||||

Listen, this whole Jesus caper has gone too far. You know how sometimes you realise that someone has misunderstood you and you know you should set them right but for some reason you just leave it alone and then the misunderstanding gets passed on to other people and they pass it on to still more and it changes form and grows and grows and then it has a whole life of its own that has nothing to do with the original incident and the prospect of sorting it all out is overwhelming but you have to try anyway because some serious shit is at stake? Yeah, well, that's what's happened here, see?

I'm not saying there was no such person as Jesus, you understand. I mean, there were scads of men with that name in my village alone. But I know, and you know, that we're not here to talk about those other men – those rabbis and rabbis' sons and craftsmen and fishermen and layabouts. Because, even though you know Jesus was a popular name in my part of the world and that it continues to be popular in other, newer parts of the world, the name really only ever refers to one man. Jesus, to you, means the Christ, the Messiah, the Saviour, the King of Kings, Light of the World, Son of God, the one and only Lord. My brother.

That last title is the only one he's earned and that's the problem. Jesus – Light of the World, King of Kings, *yada yada yada* – was born of woman, lived a short but racy life and then died a painful and humiliating death. And when I say 'died' I mean it in the full human sense of the world. Jesus is as dead as Princess Diana and Napoleon and your great-great-grandma. He's as dead as Elvis (yes, he is), Marilyn Monroe and Jimmy Dean. He's as dead as you will be someday. (Don't let that worry you by the way: I'm dead and I'm fine. Most of us are.)

Anyway, as I said, my brother Jesus was born – OK, before I can go on I have to clear something up and... well, this is hard for me to say, because she's my *mother*, you know? But even I can't pretend that a woman can have ten children without ever having, you know, *done it*. Sure, *now* it could happen because you all have the technology but back in the day there was just the old-fashioned way of getting knocked up, so... OK, enough about my mum.

Actually, no, that's not enough. See, some of you have got some weird ideas about the old girl and there's no point setting you straight about JC if you just transfer all your prayers and whatnot on to her. (JC, by the way, is what most of us up here call him nowadays. It started as a joke – we gave him heaps about the whole 'Christ' thing – but then as more and more Jesuses came through the gates it became a matter of practicality. I mean, call out 'Yo, Jesus' up here and you get a stampede, you know?)

Anyway, back to my mum, Mary. (A while back some idiots started calling her VM, thinking that was funny the way calling Jesus JC was funny. But calling someone's mother a virgin is not on a par with calling a young fella Christ and, well, my mother has a lot of sons and none of us could stand for her being disrespected like that, you know? So she's just plain Mary now, thanks very much.) Anyway, the point is that Mum is a dear but she's no more a saint than she is a virgin so you can cut out all that praying and candle-lighting.

Back to JC. He really put Mum through some serious shit in his day. You know how it is with kids – one day he's a little angel playing under Daddy's feet in the workshop and giggling while you shower him with kisses before bed, and the next he's a gangly-limbed, long-haired stranger hanging around with thieves and prostitutes and denying he's even related to you.

And JC being the charismatic, confident guy he is, well, people flocked to him. They gathered at his feet, jostled to walk alongside him, gave away their belongings and abandoned their families to go walkabout with him. There was nothing miraculous about it – weak people, people who've fucked up a lot, people who are kind of lost – those kinds of people are very attracted to confident, charismatic young guys who claim to have all the answers.

Man, it sounds like I'm saying he was a charlatan or sleazebag or something. He wasn't. He was just a sparky young fella whose popularity went to his head. It's not like I would have handled it any better. I mean, after he died I had control of his mob for a couple of years and I about choked on the power. When I think about how agitated I used to get about whether or not my followers had their todgers snipped or not I feel like a total prat. I just wanted to keep the old gang together the way it had been when JC was alive. I had no idea it would turn out like this.

Look, my brother is a super guy, truly. He's just not a super*natural* guy, if you see the difference. Lots of people don't. Lots of people talk like the fact he was kind to lepers and whores means he *must* be holy. It's weird for us old-timers, not just because we know the guy to be, well, just a *guy*, but because in our day nobody connected goodness with godliness. Deities were selfish, vain, unreasonable tyrants who would send pestilence or a flood as soon as look at you. Now everyone equates God with peace and justice despite the fact that the world is just as unfair and brutal as it ever was. The only reason they expect it to be fairer and nicer is because they think my brother promised it would be, and the only reason they think that was because this batshit crazy salesman called Saul told them so.

Look, Saul (he's gone back to his original name now – part of his attempt to pretend none of this ever happened) is nice enough, but he's a couple of locusts short of a plague, if you know what I mean. Like, he never even met my brother until he got here and that meeting was one of the least divine things I've seen in my life and death. It was also the funniest. Hearing the father of the Christian Church cry out, 'But Lord, you're supposed to love your enemies!' while said alleged Lord kicks the stuffing out of him is worth waiting eternity for, I can tell you.

To be fair, it's not all Saul's fault. If it hadn't been for those resurrection rumours, he never would have latched on to my bro's story in the first place. He probably would have decided to evangelise Artemis or someone instead. That resurrection bullshit was tough to take, man. It still is. It's not that I'm sad he didn't rise from his tomb – I mean, the dude's right here with me, so I'm cool with the fact he died. It's just that if you knew what crucifixion was like you would understand that all anybody who loved him wanted at the time was for him to be pulled down and buried in the cool earth for eternity.

They left him up there for nine days. The nails broke through the meat of his hands and what was left of his arms dropped down towards his shredded feet. By the time they took him down he was indistinguishable from a butchered cow. What they buried was a slab of meat, not a man. Did I see my dead brother walk? No. I only saw him desiccate and rot.

Like I said, he's here with me now and that makes the memory of his crucifixion easier to bear. For me, anyway. For him, it's a different story. It's like it wasn't bad enough he had to die so horribly, you lot have to keep on about it, day after day, year after year, millennium after fucking millennium.

In the early days he had a sense of humour about it. When I first got here he clapped me on the back and said, 'You had to be martyred too, didn't you, James? Always gotta copy everything I do. Tough shit, though, kid, only one messiah per family.'

He used to talk about the pranks he'd pull when his followers arrived, how he'd let them catch him on his knees worshipping

noise

John the Baptist. And when that bloke in the Arabian Desert started gathering followers, JC got all cocky, because he had a bet going with some of us that the whole Christ cult wouldn't last more than a millennium and it looked like he had won with centuries to spare. But then... Well, you know what happened then.

Look, most of us take a peek at the world of the living from time to time – eternity is a drag without new information to talk about and new events to place bets on. (We've stopped betting on political elections, by the way, so if you're electing these douches just to fuck with us you can stop now, OK?) Anyway, human beings are a damned despicable bunch much of the time, and so most of us keep our exposure to a minimum. But old JC can't keep away. I used to think he was just being vain, wanting to hear himself worshipped day and night, but then a little while ago some joker claimed to have found my ossuary and the whole little earth was buzzing with theories about me and my life, and I admit I went into full-on surveillance mode. I was big news for less than a year and I was exhausted; my brother has been dealing with far worse for two thousand years.

There's this expression some of you use: 'Jesus weeps.' Well, he does, it's true. Wouldn't you if it was your name being hollered every time a child died of cancer or a little baby was raped? Wouldn't you weep if whenever swords were pushed through squishy human flesh or men were locked in cages or women beaten with sticks or nations destroyed or sweethearts buried, someone somewhere screamed out your name?

He weeps, because you celebrate his death and decorate your houses with obscene portraits of his bloodied corpse. He weeps because in your desperate attempts to find meaning in life you have made his meaningless. He weeps because he was once a man and you have made him a symbol, which is the same as making him disappear. Jesus weeps, you selfish fuckers, because you keep on calling him to fix stuff and he can't and you won't so the pain just keeps on.

I told him I was going to tell you the truth and he just kind of shrugged. He said it won't make any difference. He said that people don't believe in something because it's true; they believe in it because they need to. Maybe that's right, because *I* believe that one day human beings are going to wake the fuck up and take responsibility for their whining, murdering, torturing selves. I need to believe that because unlike you delusional, selfish pricks I actually do love the man you call Jesus. He's my brother, OK? And I believe it's time humanity backed the fuck off.

swimsuit issue

kevin sampsell

In the summer of 1992, I was working as a DJ at a radio station in Spokane, Washington. It was an AM/FM set-up. I did the AM side on weekends, playing 'classic country' music under one name, then some fill-in shifts under a different name on the FM side, which was the town's big Top 40 station. It was a golden age of music for me. I had been through a Britpop phase in the late eighties, then dove into the whole American indie scene of the early nineties. The landscape of exciting bands was deep and good. I got into SY during their Goo/Dirty period, perhaps their poppiest days.

Anyway, I remember getting a cassette of Dirty *at a radio station picnic. A woman from Geffen Records was there and she gave me an advance copy. She talked about how it was her favourite album of the year and her enthusiasm made me believe her.*

'Swimsuit Issue' was my favourite song right away. It seemed so pointed and angry. But even when Kim was angry, her voice still exuded sexiness.

Guys just stare at my tits without shame. It doesn't matter what I wear. I'll throw something on with a plunge and my whole day is chaos. Every neck cranes freakishly, every eyeball almost popping out like fingers nervously brushing me. The sound of their breathing like an asthma ward. Slow cars cruising beside me. Some of the women have to hold themselves back. They all want to kill me.

At least I can get some service at the hardware store now. Not like ten years ago, when I was going on dates with record-store clerks and delivery men – guys who welcomed the non-threatening stature of my small sickly-looking titties. I couldn't even call them tits. I had a child's chest. Titties. A cute name. But mine were horrible and that was why I ended up smashing people's shit. I'd get fed up with everything and I didn't trust nature or God or even my friends.

When I was twenty-eight, I somehow ended up with a guy twice my age. My family gave up on me at that point. They didn't even know his name. They just called him *the old guy*, even though his name was simple, strong, standard.

Jack.

He didn't really give a shit about anything. I mean, Jack was really nice but he was a rebel, a man who couldn't be told what to do or think. He made a bunch of money working for some drug company and getting out just before they got sued for clogging up some kid's heart valve or something. They even talked about it on *60 Minutes* and when they tried to interview Jack he just smiled and said he had nothing more to do with the company. The reporter, some black lady with feathered hair poofed out like Farrah Fawcett, asked him something else and Jack stuck his hand out to block the camera and climbed into his Porsche. It was so cool. Sometimes I'll watch that clip on some website and imagine that I'm there too, in the Porsche, wearing sunglasses and a really expensive dress. And sometimes, yeah, I'll tell people I was there. The camera never gets a good shot into the car.

Besides, I have been in that car. I've been all over that car. I know what the dome light of that car feels like on the bottom of my left foot. I know the perfect way to brace myself against the leather steering wheel. I know the exact position to put the rear-view mirror so I can see all this happen. I liked to watch him do it to me, his furry back clenching and sweating. It's why they call it a rear-view mirror, I joked to him.

But he hated my titties too. He asked me if I had cancer the first time we had sex. Or at least it seemed like he was asking me that. His face made a horrible face. He screwed me real fast because he wanted to get it over with. His anguish over my body matched my own level of self-hatred. I came despite the hate, or because of it. Then he said I had a pretty face.

I shouldn't say I hate myself. That's not right. I do have a nice face. Cute hair, brown and wavy. My arms aren't gross. I'm thin around the waist and ankles. My ass is actually pretty good. I went to school. I achieved some goals. I type eighty words a minute. I can go a whole weekend alone without killing myself.

So Jack set it up for me pretty quick. Had me quit my job and send the boys to Grandma's. I didn't mention my kids yet, did I? Twin boys. Thurston and Lee, eight years old. Good kids, independent, always prowling the neighbourhood with those Hispanic kids from down the street. Those little guys are proof that I was once loved by someone my parents approved of. His name was Lesley, like a girl. Won't Lesley be surprised?

It seemed like an eternity later when I could finally remove the bandages. I dragged myself around the halls of the hospital and felt like I was taking someone else's body for a walk. Jack sent me new swimsuits every day while I healed. He said they were actual ones he saw in the swimsuit issue of a sports magazine. He couldn't wait to get me out to the beach.

I'll always remember that moment of the bandages circling off me. I watched in the mirror that the nurse held just right, so all I saw was my middle, now top heavy, ready to burst forth. It was like watching myself being born again, without a face.

It's amazing what boobs can do. It feels so weird to even say that word in regard to myself. I always used it when talking about others. Ashley's boobs. Naomi's boobs. Someone once said, *If they don't bounce, they're not boobs.* Now I bounce. Jack liked to see me bounce. He didn't want to go a night without doing something obscene to me after my operation. His enthusiasm cranked up my confidence and helped me grow into my new body. And it did feel like a whole new body. Like my tits had taken over my body.

As soon as my scars healed and I got used to the sheer mass and weight of my breasts – the almost ridiculous presence of them – I emailed an old boyfriend from ten years ago and dropped a hint about my new look. This is someone who jokingly called me 'little boy' until I started crying. We went out for a whole year and *only* had doggy-style sex. Sometimes he told me to put a T-shirt on when we did it. I think he gave me my first orgasm.

Steve emailed me back and said he was working in a music store, giving guitar lessons to kids. He told me he'd send me a guitar if I sent him photos of myself. I looked him up on the Internet and saw that he was still cute. I don't really know what I'd do with a guitar but I wanted him to see me so I asked Jack to snap some pictures of me. I didn't say anything about Steve, though I'm sure he probably wouldn't care. He talked to his old girlfriends and I didn't freak out about that.

They turned out pretty good. In one of them I'm sitting on the edge of bed, leaning over a little, the silicone working its magic, staring straight through the lens. There's a profile shot where you can really see what a nice job the surgeon did. Jack said we should send that one to the doctor. He could put that one on his business card, Jack said. We took a few in some of my new swimsuits too, and then several in the shower. Jack asked me to soap myself up. I liked touching them for the camera. I felt like I could do anything with them and they'd look good. I sent a couple of the photos to Steve and he wrote back saying they looked *sensational*. He said he wrote a song about me and wanted me to hear it. I asked for his phone number so he wouldn't call when I was with Jack. I was jittery about calling him, though, and it took me two weeks to gather the nerve.

He sounded the same as he always did when he answered. Really sweet but with a nasty temper buried somewhere. He asked if I was sending more photos and who took the ones he'd already seen. I lied to him and told him a girlfriend had taken them. Stacey, I said her name was. She had hers done too, I said for some reason. We talked for about an hour. He'd ask about my parents and my kids and my life but the discussion always ended up on my tits. Or *breasts*, as Steve first called them. It took him a few cautious moments to warn up to *tits*, but then he really enjoyed saying it. What did your parents say about them? What do your kids think about them? Sometimes it was like he was interviewing just my tits.

Finally, he played me his song. He set his phone down next to where he was, picked up his guitar and started serenading me. He stopped halfway. *Can you hear me?* he yelled down at the phone. Yes, I shouted back. He continued his song. Over the phone it sounded like a fuzzy old radio. Some of the words were hard to make out. There was a part where he said something about my face looking hard or maybe he was saying my face made him hard. I didn't want to ask. By the time he got to the third verse I was able to ignore the terrible melody and focus on the words. They dripped with nostalgia, regret and horniness. I asked him to sing it again and I touched myself as he did. I couldn't quite bring myself off but it was enough for me just knowing that he wanted to have sex with me again.

The next day, he sent me an email saying that he was *thrilled, maybe too thrilled,* to have talked to me. He wrote a description of the kinds of photos he wanted me to send next and asked if he could see a photo of my friend Stacey as well. I responded and told him Stacey wouldn't do it. He sent me a snippy reply, one that was rude and all business. Something like: 'Talk to Stacey some more and tell her I'll make it worth her while. And send me some photos of you with your wig.'

I had told him, while on the phone, about buying a wig after the operation. I didn't say anything about Jack wanting to see me with long blonde hair. I didn't say anything about Jack at all. I said something dumb like, *I'm just into having fun now.* To him it probably sounded like, *I'll hump anything with a penis.* Anyway, I so happen to have a couple of wig shots. I sent them to him. I titled the email: 'Say Hello to Your New Blonde Goddess'.

After that, Steve insisted on calling the blonde me by a different name. *Letecia.*

I started to have panic attacks and stopped emailing with Steve. Jack was getting more possessive and I was starting to worry he'd find out.

One night at dinner, Jack said he wanted to get me liposuction. Imagine yourself with fifteen pounds chopped off, he said. You'd be a knockout. I thought it was a weird thing to talk about at dinner but I was happy. I knew that if Jack was spending that kind of money on me it meant that he really loved me. He wanted to make it easy on me and I felt my heart swell and lift. I felt like I couldn't breathe for a moment and when I saw tears form in his eyes, I started crying too. I touched his face and he leaned forward into my hand. He moved to kiss me and his hands moved over my breasts so gently. My *breasts*. I don't mind that word right now, at this moment. It seems right and pure. They were warm to his touch. Always warm.

But the next morning, I realised that I didn't want another surgery. I looked over at Jack as he slept. He had wrinkles, spots, grey bristly hair. Sometimes I forgot what he looked like when he wasn't around. I'd imagine him as a superior being, a master of life, of getting things done. He got things done for me. But what about him? I never noticed that hair growing out of his ears. The weird lines all over his neck. Not wrinkles really, but lines. Like graph paper. I smelled his neck. It smelled like Band-Aids. My eyes and nose circled his head slowly as he wheezed. Sometimes when he slept he made so much noise it was like he was fighting with someone. There were age spots on his scalp. His hair barely survived there. He was too tan. I wondered if he'd get cancer. I pulled the sheets back and looked down on his body. He had half of a morning hard-on but it was hard to notice under the girth of his belly. His belly button the size of a quarter. I reached over to my purse and took a quarter out. I set it there and it fell inside. For a moment I wondered how far it went. Did it actually disappear in there? Would he carry that quarter around for a few days before noticing it?

I got out of bed quietly. I picked some clothes out of the closet and took off my pyjamas quietly. There was a full-length mirror on the closet door. It was a double door, so the mirror was actually in two pieces. In one mirror, I looked at myself naked for a couple of slow minutes. In the other mirror, I watched Jack sleep, the covers pulled down. I wondered if he would wake up if I stared at him long enough. I slowly got dressed, trying to stare at him without blinking. My eyes started to hurt. I finally left the room, closing the door softly. I walked by the boys' room and they were already up and gone. It was a school day. A warm, promising, no clouds in the sky kind of day. I opened the front door and felt the sun on my skin. It lit up my body and I felt good. I slammed the door right then and there.

kool thing; or why i want to fuck patty hearst

tom mccarthy

I remember, in 1992 or so, listening to Kim Gordon's voice monologuing over 'Kool Thing'. She was talking about a white girl lying on a bed with a dagger in her hand, staring at a black panther in a tree; and she said it had something to do with Patty Hearst. I didn't know who Patty Hearst was then. Years later, when I visited the Joyce Museum in the gun-tower where he spent the night that Ulysses *emerged from, there was a life-sized black panther in the bedroom: Joyce's roommate, like his hero Stephen's, had a nightmare with one in it and, picking a gun up in his half-sleep from the night-table beside his bed, fired it over Joyce's head. Beneath the bedroom was a storeroom for gunpowder; in past centuries the guardians of the tower had to be careful not to*

*generate any sparks. Maybe all avant-gardes begin
with gunpowder and a dream of a black panther.*

|||||||||||||||||||||||||||||||

I imagine her standing in a bathrobe and alpaca slippers, her hair still wet from the shower, her fingers sticky from the home-made pastry she's been rolling on her kitchen counter. I imagine peering at her through the front door's frosted glass, her face distending as she moves behind it; or how it looks from her side, the figures dark and imprecise against the night, the stick-shapes by their waists she doesn't know are guns. Or later, after they've knocked her down and carted her off to their hideout, the way she squints through a black eye at the TV screen, watching the news, seeing the building where she lived all cordoned off by police tape, reporters crowded round her mother, who wears black, and thinking: *No, that's wrong, it's she who's dead, not me. My father standing beside her is dead as well. And the detectives, anchormen and commentators, the others too, everyone behind the screen: all distant, unreal, dead.*

I picture her sitting in the closet with its musty carpet and rubber-foam mattress, its soundproofing pads that smell of old sweat, listening to the radio they've placed there with her, listening hour after hour, like Orphée, as the song lyrics, bulletins and station idents run together, all the voices blurring: disc jockeys, announcers, lonely night-time callers. I hear her solitude in theirs, and theirs in hers, and in both of these the solitude of fur-trappers and gold-prospectors, bums and travelling salesmen, taxi drivers and nightwatchmen, a continental loneliness booming

and echoing through centuries. And behind all these, I hear
the solitude of her own grandfather: the only child, estranged
husband, jealous sugar-daddy, would-be president who couldn't
get the people to like him enough to elect him so had his own
world built for him to rule over and peopled it with elephants
and zebras, lions, tigers, tahr goats, monkeys; filled its dining
halls and billiard rooms with gargoyles, frescoes, tapestries and
kantharoses; obliged his guests to watch each evening the films,
still unreleased, that he'd produced; forced them to wear fancy
dress so they would all stay behind masks; forbade them to speak
of death, which made the word hang in the air unspoken all the
time; stayed up long after they and all the butlers, gardeners,
gamekeepers and switchboard operators had gone to sleep and,
reclining on his four-poster beneath a painting of Napoleon
alone before the Sphinx, would drift off to the sound of panthers
shrieking in the night.

I imagine her hairs bristling as she tells her parents that they're
bourgeois pigs and that she'll never come back home; her voice
crackling with excitement as she reads on to a tape the revolutionary
statement that will soon be played on every radio and television
station in the country. I see her eyes blaze like coal fires as she poses
with a machine gun in front of the Egyptian symbol painted on the
wall: the seven-headed cobra Wadjet, Lady of Devouring Flame,
Wadjet the Invincible, whose presence causes malachite to glisten,
she who lives according to her will, the pupil in the eye of Re the
sun, who hisses: *Few approach me. The confederacy of Seth is at my
side and what is near me burns.*

I picture her as the heroine of the pulp-porn novel published
several years before her kidnapping in which a black man steals

a debutante named Patricia, locks her in a hideaway and has his way with her until the Negro semen pickling her brain makes her a criminal. I wonder whether her kidnappers had read it, then realise that it doesn't matter: it's all fiction, the whole thing. I tell myself she understands this, and that she's letting the story play itself out by assuming the main role.

I picture her as Tania, Che's lover; as Ophelia the teenage suicide; as Antigone the goth; as Sylvia Plath, panther-stalked girl who never had a gun placed in her hands but stuck her head inside an oven; as Molly Bloom, who lies in bed bleeding, thinking of all the men she's had; as Stephen Dedalus, boy-Cordelia who hears the ruin of all space, shattered glass and toppling masonry, and time one livid final flame; as James Joyce himself, who summoned it all up from a dream of a black panther; or as his favourite child Lucia, the mad spark who cracked under the weight of her inheritance. I picture her as the Statue of Liberty holding a stick of dynamite instead of a torch. I picture her as Lara Croft, raider of tombs, running through urban landscapes out of Eldridge Cleaver: armoured vehicles criss-crossing city streets, black smoke billowing against the daylight sky, the sound of tommy guns and snipers' rifles, barbed wire closing off whole sections of the city, 'and everywhere the smell of cordite'.

I see her riding in a car through San Francisco with the window wound down, breeze tickling her hair and flapping her donkey jacket's collar, the untinned air and clear blue daylight making her giddy; then running from the car into a bank, shouting her name out as she waves her gun at terrified customers and staff. I picture the movements of the other revolutionaries as they vault the counters, throw open the cash drawers; the cascade of glass as the bullet-peppered windows crystallise and fall; the screech of the car's tyres as it pulls off again; and her, staring back through the rear window as the bank and street and people drain away and the world retreats again behind a screen.

Like Orphée through the silver mirror: Patty in the Zone. I see her multiplying into a thousand different women as the hotlines set up in her name jam up with calls reporting sightings of her in supermarkets, cinemas and cafés, pool halls, libraries and trains. She's morphing from a typist in Louisiana to a hitchhiker in Tennessee, a croupier in Vegas, Sacramento dancer, toll-collector on the Arizona interstate, a hundred New York students, seven hundred California teenagers – and splitting further in kaleidoscopes of fantasies and dreams, her image broken down to arsenals of double-gauges, thirty-calibres and twelve-bores, grenades and pipe bombs, angles of limbs on shadows of assassins climbing staircases at night. And she becomes some of these images, some of the characters as well: dressing as an airline stewardess, a hotel clerk, a secretary – or, when she and her comrades leave San Francisco for Los Angeles, a jazz musician, face blacked up and instrument case full of weapons. I see her looking at the traffic on the freeway, playing with the radio, always the radio, hearing revolutionary subtexts in the songs and sympathetic propaganda in the interference between broadcast areas; then, cruising round Watts and Compton, seeing the ruined houses and the gutted buses, thinking: *Yes, this is the Zone, and it's begun, the final uprising, the crisis, the denouement.*

I understand she has to miss it, like a lead player wandering offstage in some anxious dream and getting waylaid among props and curtain-ropes. There's a *correctness* in her decision to go shopping for provisions just before the police swoop on the house with armoured cars; and in the way she hears it, on the radio (where else?); and the way she checks into a Disneyland motel and turns the TV on to see the house go up in flames, one of her friends run out and have her lungs ripped from her chest by bullets, blood shoot backwards from another's head, the rest burning inside, the angle changing slightly with each channel. I picture her biting her hand to stifle screams, the make-up running down her face, her body bouncing on the bed, and think: this is the Patty Hearst I want to fuck – not the chat-show guest or irony-trophy movie extra she became, but this one here. I want to fuck this one because this one's America: all of it, sitting in a motel bedroom, watching the apocalypse on television.

unmade bed

christopher coake

I first heard Sonic Youth in college, like everyone else. This was 1992, and the song I heard was '100%'. I didn't know what to make of it, though I appreciated that it was loud. I valued loud, then.

But in 1992 I was only a year removed from having seen (and enjoyed) a triple-bill concert featuring Cinderella, Extreme, and David Lee Roth (who'd ridden an inflatable microphone around the stage like a rodeo bronco). After hearing '100%' I tried to listen to a friend's copy of Daydream Nation, *and I have to admit that, in college, my mind wide open, during a seminal time in alternative music history, I was bewildered. I didn't get Sonic Youth. Nirvana, Pearl Jam – grunge was just barely understandable to me. Sonic Youth was a little… noisy.*

But I was slow, musically. I grew up in rural Indiana, where 'classic rock', as transmitted by radio station WFBQ, reigns o'er all. In college I once admitted in print (I had a column in the newspaper) that I thought Aerosmith was cutting-edge.

So consider this story penance for that old column. For blithely passing by a pretty great time in American music and not paying attention. I get Sonic Youth now. In the same way that my tastes and ambitions in literature have deepened and expanded, so have I come to appreciate music of all kinds, especially the noisy kind.

I'm not a snob. My iPod still holds music from Cinderella and Extreme and even Aerosmith (early Aerosmith. Please). But it's also got Daydream Nation. And Sonic Nurse – which, actually, was the first Sonic Youth album I owned; from there I went backward, snapping up all I could. 'Unmade Bed' was the song that first made me perk up my ears. My point of entry.

I got to see Sonic Youth perform, in Reno, while I was writing this story. (Afterward I got to shake Thurston's hand, all the while sure I was coming across as a guy who had once praised 'Janie's Got A Gun' in his college newspaper.) I was with my friend Mike, who is an accomplished drummer, a man whose childhood was steeped in classic rock himself, and who had been, hitherto, a Sonic Youth neophyte. The show had left us reeling. It was beautiful and absorbing, sure. But then one particular wave of feedback was so loud it made me break out in sweat. Mike and I stared at each other in awe. I think that was when I truly understood.

Take it from a former Hoosier farm kid, who
means it as the highest compliment:
Sonic Youth rock.

||||||||||||||||||||||||||||||||

Tim's mouth finally shuts. He's said what he came to say and, now that it's said, he understands: he's made a bad mistake. Kurt stands up from the bar and faces him. The guys drinking with Kurt, their faces go hard and cold, and they stand up too. They're all the same, all like Kurt: big and beery and mean. Country mean, slit-eyed mean. Desert mean. *Yeah,* Kurt says, and comes for him. Tim ought to run, but things are happening too quickly, and he's still a little – a lot – drunk, and then Kurt's right in front of him, and it's too late. Kurt's friends don't move. Like they know he doesn't need any help, this time. Why would he? Tim looks like the man he is: a skinny guy who doesn't work out and who doesn't make money with his hands and his muscles. He couldn't be more different from these men. He doesn't do his drinking at the Sawdust Bar. He's not tanned into creases and leather. He doesn't use too much hair gel, doesn't go drinking in steel-toed work boots or blue jeans with paint crusted across the thighs. One of Kurt's hands grabs up the front of Tim's shirt in a knot, and any courage Tim might have had a few seconds ago – it wasn't much – drains right out the soles of his feet, when Kurt pulls him up off them, one armed. Kurt's other hand squeezes Tim's chin. Tim thought he could do this with resilience. With guts, a little guile. He's smarter than Kurt. He's in the right. Those things ought to matter. On the way over to the Sawdust he imagined himself striding through the parking lot, into the bar, saying what he had to say. Jabbing a finger into Kurt's chest. Then what? He'd kick Kurt in the balls. He'd pick up a beer bottle or a pool cue. Stand over Kurt's whimpering body and say *Don't call her again.* But now Kurt's hand on his chin is rough and solid and unyielding as granite. Kurt's eyes squint. *You,* he says, *are fucked.* And Tim believes him. He's made plenty of other mistakes in his life, and it could fairly be said that sleeping with Kurt's girl was a big one, but this, this is the worst he could do: driving more than a little drunk down back streets into Sparks, to the Sawdust Bar, wobbling into the dark stinking insides, finding Kurt, who he'd only ever seen in pictures, and then saying what he said – *Leave her alone, Kurt* – watching Kurt nodding to himself, finishing his beer, not even looking up, while Tim went on like a dumbfuck – *Kathy's a good woman, she deserves better, so just leave her the fuck alone, let her live her life* – seeing a weird energy in Kurt, a tense set to his shoulders, like this is what he's been hoping for all night, every night: for the guy Kathy's slept with to show up in front of him. For a chance to slam down his bottle on the bar and stand up and let that crazy look take over his square, tanned face. To grab Tim's shirt and grunt into his face what he does now: *Who the fuck are you?* Like he's been practising it. He's so obviously deranged, meanness and hatred swinging out from his eyes like a slap, that Tim answers him, stupidly: *I'm Tim Randall.* Like Kurt gives any little shit. Tim sees in Kurt's eyes: he will always and forevermore be nothing but the skinny little faggot who fucked Kathy. Whatever he was before coming through the door, that's over now. And what is he, anyway? He's Timothy Brian Randall. A name that says nothing at all: no promise, nothing exceptional. Look at him. He's thirty years old and he works in a clothing store. He's not simply a worker there, but he's not quite a manager either. He has a key to the register but not to the safe. He's well dressed because of the job, but because of that job he'll never be cool. He lives in Reno in an old hotel called Archer's Nugget, not a casino like the seven other Nuggets in town, though you can go downstairs and play video poker at the bar, which is where Tim does his drinking – and which is where, a few weeks back, he made the first of the many mistakes that would lead him to this last one. Where he started drinking with Kathy. *Sit down,* he said to her. *What can I get you?* She said, *You don't have to buy me a drink.* He said, *No, but I really want to.* If he'd left out the *really.* Kurt's breathing hisses between his tight pale lips. The bar at Archer's Nugget is done up in old plush red velvet and the people who drink in there are almost all residents – most of them elderly folks, Old Reno, wearing string ties and beehive hairdos, Old Reno afraid to walk outside into New Reno, which is new and young and clueless and mostly from California. Like Tim. Kurt's not Old or New Reno. He's Country. He's desert-dry. Hard-eyed like a lizard. Tim knows from Kathy: Kurt drives a pick-up truck and hates Mexicans and on weekends drives up on to Peavine Peak with his friends to shoot old refrigerators. He works out obsessively and likes Toby Keith and would be in the Marines if he didn't have one leg shorter than the other. He's also got a tiny dick. Kathy told him that, too. Kurt swings Tim one hundred and eighty degrees and starts to give him the bum's rush around the end of the bar – where there's a door under a half-lit sign that says only IT. *A teeny, tiny, little dick.* The small of Tim's back hits the doorknob. The bartender's looking away, a little smile: help's not coming. For the first time in Tim's life he's going to get a full-on beating. Maybe worse. Kurt's capable, Tim can feel it in his hands, in the speed they're travelling. And Tim goes limp. He gives in. He feels like he's behind the wheel of a car spinning out of control on ice. *I worry sometimes he might kill me,* Kathy said. *I know he's hit other girls.* Girls, she said, like she's still one herself, like there aren't grown-up consequences for what she's done. Cold air now, they're out the door and into a dark lot which, like the bar itself, is under an overpass, so dark Tim can barely see Kurt's sneering face. Kathy lay down next to Tim in his bed, in his tiny room on the third floor of Archer's Nugget. He woke up from a nap to the sound of her key in the door. He'd been dreaming of the devil, in whom he doesn't believe, leering at him; he almost screamed. Then she was in the room. Perfume, almost peppery. *It's OK,* she said, *I have a key, I'm sorry, I didn't know where to go right now.* They'd shared, at that time, not much. A conversation or two. A couple of beers. Six weeks ago, he walked into her office in the lobby to pay his weekly rent. He knew her then only as the gorgeous woman he handed his cheque to, who smiled at him because it was her job. But this time he saw she'd been crying. She said, *Hi, Tim,* and he was surprised she even knew his name; women like her historically didn't. *You OK?* he asked. *You're a guy,* she said. *Listen to this.* She played him a message from the answering machine on her desk. He was a guy; he was reminded every time he saw Kathy, paying his rent. She's tall, lush, she has long rust-red hair. Wears too much make-up. A dark line drawn around her glistening lips. Wide green eyes, a big white smile. Very smart black suits with low necklines. Freckles on her breastbone. All Tim knew about her then was that he guessed she had some self-esteem, to be working in that office, when she could make twice her pay as a cocktail waitress a few streets over. *Listen*, she said, and pressed the button. And then the voice of Kurt. *Come here, asshole*, he says to Tim now, even though Tim's already clutched close enough to him to smell the beer on his breath. *Kath*, Kurt said on the machine. *Kath, I don't know about this. It's too much. All right? I mean, you're great, you are, but – look, I don't know. I just don't know.* Tim sat in the office with Kathy, patting her hand while she cried. *Sounds final to me*, he said, like he knew what the fuck he was talking about. She said, *I just… I love him, and I mentioned it would, you know, be nice to have a house, a place of our own, and I was so stupid, I said, imagine you and me, living like that, and Kurt got all like stiff and then this and I –* And Tim said, *Hey, would a drink help? My treat?* And then three weeks and a few beers later she's sitting on the edge of his bed, she's opened his door with her key. *I trust you*, she says. She kicks off her shoes. *Don't get up*, she says. *I just need a cuddle.* A cuddle. Tim slips his arm around her. He's never been with a woman in this bed. He hasn't slept with any woman anywhere since leaving California. Since Becky left him. Since in her wake he moved from Sacramento to the Biggest Little City in the World and rented a room in Archer's Nugget and got a job selling off-the-rack suits. Why Reno? Why not? He had to go someplace, and Becky never liked it here. He had, did, does: the desert and the mountains and the skies going orange at dusk. The gaudy Christmas-light sparkle of the downtown. Putting a quarter in a slot machine, to see whether the breakfast he just ate came for free. The prospect of some kind of story, some kind of adventure. Luck touching his shoulder a second time in his life. A sound comes out of Kurt's throat now, a rising growl, and Tim's going even faster. Kurt drives him backwards into one of the pillars of the overpass.

Harder than Tim's ever hit anything. His head cracks against the concrete and the world goes tilted. He's fucked. Tim would hit Kurt now if he could but everything's fuzzy and sideways and he can't clench his fists. Kurt whispers at his ear, intimate like a girl in a bed, but the words make no sense, his head's full of a white light like a new-struck match. *He left me for good*, Kathy says, in his arms. Cuddling. *He's in Lovelock now. Probably with that bitch Luann. I was sad, and then I remembered what you said the other day. You're right. I can do anything I want, I'm free.* He did say that. It's true. *There's no reason I can't be here*, she says. *I spent my whole life doing what people want. What Kurt wants. But what if I want you? There's no law against it.* Her breath is hot and damp, the breath of tears. Her skirt sizzles across her stockings. *I'm not going to say his name again*, she says. A few minutes later they're both naked below the waist, she's running a lacquered nail up and down the length of him, his head full of light, and she says, *Kurt's got a teeny, tiny dick. I pretended I didn't care.* Kurt drops him to the ground, into cold wet muck. Tim can't see him. Kurt kicks him: a stabbing pain in his ribs, but distant. Like something he dreams. Steel-toed boots. It hurts far away and up close: worse than he can do anything about. Kathy lifts Tim's hand and slips it between her legs. He shouldn't be thinking of Kathy. He should be thinking of Becky. His wife. Now that his life's over: the love of his life. *You're a shit*, Becky says to him. She has to say it; he cheated on her. The old song: a girl at the office. Twenty-two and half-Korean and a sad newlywed, who, one night, after Tim said, *No marriage is easy*, asked him, *Yours too?* He lied, said *Yes*, and all of a sudden it was the truth. Becky's right, she always was. He's a shit. He pledged his life to her. He meant it. She came down the aisle and he would have given her the bleeding heart from his chest instead of a ring. Words. Kurt kneels next to him and says, *That bitch. You? You?* Every time he says *you* he slaps down at Tim's face. *Jesus, Kathy, some little faggot shit like this? Huh?* A shit, he says. Everyone's of the same mind. Tim curls on his side in the muck. When he was a kid he used to want to be an astronomer. He had a telescope. Saw the Pleiades. But then he realised it was all just math. Then he wanted to be a politician, but he can't speak in public; his knees shake. He studied in business. At least he could make money. At least he could love, could settle down. Then he wanted to be married, to Becky, with her little horn-rim glasses and her thick, black hair and her crooked smile. He loved her. Not enough. He whispered to a friend about the girl at work, who was getting complicated, and the friend tapped the picture of Becky on his desk and said, *Show me a pretty woman, and I'll show you a man who's tired of fucking her.* But Tim wasn't tired of it, he never was. Then that girl in his office put his hand to her breast, said, *Keep me company,* and it seemed like not very much to ask, not very much to do, he told himself just this once, he had a choice and he made it, and now he's not married any more and not one of these women loves him, and he doesn't believe in much of anything except drinking in the bar of the Nugget, and drinking more up in his room, like tonight, opening a bottle of whiskey and thinking of Kathy naked on the same bed where he sat, Kathy whispering in his ear, Kathy who the night before stood in the doorway of his room saying, *It was just a mistake, a big mistake,* and Kurt kicks his thigh and it goes numb, and then something else, like a rush of wind, and there's a long empty pause with nothing in his head but the sound of his own gasps, and then ending it is another match-strike and then his mouth is full of blood, his head full of cotton and nails and Kathy says, *Kurt's taking me back*, like she's done something wrong and needs to be forgiven, and then she says *I was wrong, he wasn't with Luann, so, um, I was kind of cheating*, he's trying to spit out a breath through the blood, Kathy says, *It was really nice, you're really nice*, her face closed off, closed down, but that first night in his room, she's gasping, skirt hitched around her waist and bunched in his hands and she kisses him long and deep and tastes like rum and tears and says, *You're better than he was, you're better in every way*, and a year and forever before Becky says, *What happened to the man who'd die before making me sad?* and Kathy says, *You've been a rock for me*, gripping him harder and harder, *I've always wanted the bad guy and now here's a good one*, he's choking and sputtering, Kurt's voice a mutter overhead like weather, like the clouds, the sun over the blanket in the pine trees where Tim first put his hand on Kathy's – Becky's! – thigh, *Tim, don't*, Kathy says, and then Kurt's face is close to his again and he's saying something Tim can't hear, and Kathy says almost in a fury like she's on stage pouring out her guts, *I love him and I always have, I can't just tell my heart what to do* and Becky says, *You shit, you spineless shit*, and the girl at the office says, *If all you're going to do is cry you better go* and he's huddled in his room just a few hours ago, crying, drinking, dialling Becky's number for the first time in months, listening to her phone ring and ring, and then a man answers, and then it's too late to be going out, and then he's at Kathy's door and she answers with a bruise on her cheek, and she says, *Don't look at me like that*, and then he's pushing her down on her bed and pulling at her jeans and she says, *You're drunk, this isn't you*, but it is, it is, he can't make her understand, *Keep me company*, says the girl's voice, and Kathy says, *Please don't* and *I won't tell you* and *He's at the Sawdust but don't go, don't be stupid, he doesn't have to know who you are* and she's crying and naked delivering her speech and he's saying, *Why are you so stupid* and she's saying, *I don't know I don't know* and Kurt's kneeling and baring his teeth and bringing down his fist and on the phone the man Tim doesn't know says, *Don't call here, I know who you are,* and Kathy's saying, *Tim, don't* and he's choking and spitting, his insides hot and cold and Kurt's shouting and his face is pressed down into the muck against Kathy's breast and he's saying, *How could you* and she's crying into her hands, saying, *If I knew how to make my heart just stop, don't you think I would?*

radical adults lick godhead style

peter wild

For maybe three weeks, morning, noon and night, all I listened to was 'Radical Adults Lick Godhead Style'. Odd lyrics (I am dead by the beauty of strangers) lodged in my head (in horror my eyehead transforms them) at random angles (into smiling, beatific room-mates) like shards of glass (from dust to dust they create rock n roll). You see. The thing about Sonic Youth, for me, is this: they're, like, the last great hoary bastion of countercultural rock. There's a line from certain sixties bands (like, say, the MC5) right to their door. But that's not all. There's something quantum about their sound. They really get to the root of things. So. I was listening to the song and the words and the guitar squall were pinging about like photons and, somehow or other, the story you're about to read bubbled up...

||||||||||||||||||||||||||||

Any external or social action, unless it's based on expanded consciousness, is robot behaviour.

Tim Leary

||||||||||||||||||||||||||||||

It takes five seconds, brothers and sisters.

One…

Alfie Vedder became untethered shortly after stepping out of the Highland-green Ford Mustang parked askance, motor running, on Warren and Forest.

Two…

He looked up once at the nearest street light, which wasn't a street light any more given that it'd been smashed out in the riots, and he shook his head, even as he fumbled in his pocket for the Zippo.

Three…

He retrieved the bottle from the interior of the car, his partner Tuck saying *Getonwithit* from the shadows on the driver's side, sparked up the lighter and lit the rag shoved like a gag in the bottle's neck.

Four…

Rag lit, he stepped and he jogged and he stepped and he jogged and he grunted and he hurled the flaming bottle across the street, a glorious clumsy parabola that he didn't stay to watch, too busy was he climbing back into the Mustang, sense drowned out in the engine roar.

162

Five…

The bottle struck the window of the Detroit office of the Committee to End the War in Vietnam, bottle and window shattering as one, the petrol igniting with the *whoomph* of a shaggy, jowly dog, the office lit, momentarily, as if it was daytime, only for the sudden lick and tickle of flame to dispel any such misconception.

Four…

He steps and he jogs, his head and his shoulders moving backwards even as he jerks forwards, building momentum, ready to throw but not yet, one more step and one more jog and still one more step and still one more jog – but then, there he was, left behind like a shoe sucked up in the mud, his socked foot still moving forward even as *he* remained behind.

And there he stood, if he could be said to stand, rooted in the middle of Warren and Forest, untethered in the heart of Detroit, sometime approximately tennish, on this, the 31st of December in the year of our Lord nineteen hundred and sixty-eight.

He was aware of himself, splinters of himself, moving off in different directions as if it was he who had suddenly shattered and not the window. Where once there had been a single Highland-green Ford Mustang, there were now two: one leaving north and one reversing south, both departing, albeit one into the future and one into the past.

His future self, his future self and Tuck, his partner of thirteen years, were on their way to the Grande Ballroom, on the corner of Boulevard and Joy, the intention being to plant evidence in the car of John Sinclair, poet, firebrand and MC5 manager, to implicate him in the firing of the office on Warren and Forest, the idea being that if Sinclair were seen as someone who was looking to create dissent from within, if Sinclair was discredited, all the better for the forces of law and order, dissenting voice that Sinclair was, thorn in their side. The MC5 were playing the Grande Ballroom that evening and Sinclair was bound to be there. Sinclair and all his White Panther cronies, all the radicals, all the Motherfuckers, all the Weathermen, all the students, all the hippies and the deadbeats and the bikers and the losers, they would all be there, in the Grande Ballroom when they took Sinclair down. The plan was to plant incriminating evidence in his car and then, as soon as that was done, take him down, through fair means or foul, whatever it took. So they were driving, his future self and Tuck, and Tuck was talking about how he planned to ask Josie, his girlfriend of eight years, to marry him, how he was going to go ask his future father-in-law for her hand at the weekend, on Sunday, he had it all planned out, what he was going to say, how the old man would take it, everything. The old man was a cancerous bastard, so Tuck said, but it didn't hurt to do things right, now, did it? You did things right, you set yourself in good stead for the future. That was how he saw it. His future self didn't speak, felt nauseous, kept repeating, in his mind, what he'd done, firebombing the Detroit office of the Committee to End the War in Vietnam; was surprised by himself, because he'd done much worse in his time, much worse, but for some reason he was troubled, felt like there was a line and he'd just stepped over it. He was over the line now and, as they moved farther and farther away from Warren and Forest so he, the future self, drew farther and farther away from the line and thereby farther and farther into uncharted, uncomfortable territory.

His previous, historical self grew happier the farther the car receded from Warren and Forest. Could be his previous self wasn't looking forward to firebombing the Detroit office of the Committee to End the War in Vietnam. The greater the distance between where he was and Warren and Forest, the greater the weight that appeared to lift off the shoulders of his previous self. Back at the field office on Michigan Avenue, the two of them zipped through a briefing, just the two of them at first but then they were joined by various members of the team, other agents and operatives, the head of their team, briefly, in and out, flitting like a summer fly, the group of them immersed in various slides and files and tape recordings running backwards through a history of supposed insurrection, from the obvious solution through a counter-intuitive list of the various challenges and obstacles they all faced, as a team, as a department, as a function of the United States federal government. Earlier and still earlier, he was eating a PB&J at his desk, transcribing surveillance tapes wearing the cushiony cans, catching up with Sinclair's movements for the previous week, and not just Sinclair, Kramer and Tyner too. Sinclair, Kramer and Tyner and all their little girlfriends and all their White Panther cronies, they were all being watched and followed and photographed and recorded and spied on and discussed, at the most senior levels, in intimate detail. He was sitting there, his previous self, at his desk in the office where everyone was dressed like it was 1955 despite the fact that out there, in the street that he could glimpse from the window beside his desk, it was 1968. The thirteen-year lag between where he sat and where he could see, the lag he spent much of his life considering when he wasn't considering right and wrong, right and wrong occupying him both in the office and at home, when he got home, which wasn't often, hiked out on jobs until late most evenings, relaxing in bars as much as he ever could relax, sleeping in his car when he could sleep or on Tuck's couch, avoiding his narrow kitchenette when he could, denying the life he spent there, the loneliness, the silly mistakes.

Three…

The future self arrived, parking on Boulevard, shuffling along Joy past the line of black-and-whites, the Detroit police out in force, so many penguins huffing and chuckling, bristling as they went by, the two of them, his future self and Tuck, wanting to lay in and start something but knowing they couldn't, wanting to lay everything from Belle Isle through to the riots at their door, at the door of the FBI, but not one of them having the guts to say anything. Russ Gibb, the proprietor of the Grande Ballroom, was poised in the doorway talking to the doorman, poised like he'd been waiting for them in his Harold Lloyd rims and his ridiculous pith helmet. *Gentlemen, gentlemen, gentlemen,* Gibb said, stepping towards them, arms outstretched like a confused dancer. *Gentlemen.* His shaken future self replied, stately, said, *Mr Gibb,* as if that was enough. *Will you be partaking of our entertainment this evening?* Gibb asked them. A look flashed between Vedder and Tuck. Something along the lines of: *Reconnoitre now, plant evidence later.* Tuck nodded and wondered aloud if the Ballroom was busy. Gibb clapped his hands like a sugared-up child and cooed, said, *Oh yes oh yes oh yes, very definitely, very definitely. Very busy indeed.* At which point Tuck and his future self pushed by, Gibb raising his voice a notch to ensure they heard: *You've missed the Psychedelic Stooges, I'm afraid, but you're still in plenty of time for the main attraction…*

Jolted from wakefulness to sleep, plunging into gunpowder dreams, gunpowder dreams haunted by the face of Viola Liuzza and the voice of Hoover saying, THE PURPOSE OF COUNTERINTELLIGENCE IS DISRUPTION; IT IS IMMATERIAL WHETHER FACTS EXIST TO SUBSTANTIATE CHARGES. His historical self grew lighter the greater the distance between the different versions of himself but still heaviness persisted. The gunpowder dreams offered a nightly record: a day here spent retrieving libel about the Republic of New Africa, a day there spent dismantling forged correspondence from the Student Nonviolent Coordinating Campaign; his mouth enlarged, warm and wet against a telephone receiver, sucking back whispered treachery from the ears of parents and landlords, strong-arming police so they wouldn't perjure themselves against dissidents, destroying fabricated evidence, confirming activists in their actions, repealing every push and shove, yanking words off arrest sheets, freeing people from the grinding machine of law, driving them away and plunging them, often violently, into the melee of protest; disorganising younger operatives, masterminding plots to dissipate infiltration in the Students for a Democratic Society and the Black Panthers; stirring up peace and social order, making sure activists were free to speak their minds, deleting hours of tape, blanking hundreds of pages of transcribed conversation, so many photographs dissolving, images whitening out in the darkroom glare. For days and weeks and months he rarely set foot in his home, putting in the hours to dilute the government's case, listening excitedly through crackles and whispers for the report of revolution, for the threat and the promise, for the date and the time. But doubting. All the while doubting. Maintaining a strong front through all the hours of daylight, through all the hours of wakefulness and then sleeping and dreaming gunpowder dreams.

Inside the ballroom, tugging, someone tugging at his hand, stopping, easing him around, a grinning girl, couldn't be more than eighteen, looked like she'd fallen off the cover to *In Watermelon Sugar*. *He who has no faith*, she said, eyes afire and hands raised as if offering invisible fruit, *and no wisdom and whose soul is in doubt – is lost*. His future self blinked slowly like a cow. He noticed the music blaring, some furious, honking harmonica goose. A Jagger-not-Jagger singing, *FROM YOUR SWIMMING POOL TO YOUR BIG CAR TO THAT SENSELESS BOMB SHELTER IN YOUR BACKYARD. For neither this world*, the girl continued, *nor the world to come nor joy is ever for the man who doubts*. He almost but not quite placed his face in her upturned palms. Her expression mutated like candle-flame: her smile fading and sparking, her eyes flaring, malevolent, beatific, thrilling, her bright white teeth shining in the dark. The music changed – a voice, *THE UNIVERSE IS PERMEATED WITH THE ODOUR OF KEROSENE*, a scream, a crunching, crunching guitar riff that sounded like some kid seesawing abuse at his mother. *Kill therefore*, she spoke over the noise with a clarity that was angelic, *kill with the sword of wisdom the doubt born of ignorance that lies in thy heart*. He wanted to speak but the words died in his throat. The girl saw, both the effort and the failure, and placed her hands gently against his cheeks, intent, a mother searching her child's face for the bee-sting left in the skin. *He who has faith has wisdom*, she said, *who lives in self-harmony, whose faith is in life; and he who finds wisdom soon finds the peace supreme*. He dry swallowed again, and then again. *The peace supreme*. That was what he wanted. Had the song changed? *I*

REALLY DON'T KNOW WHEN OR WHERE TO GO. I CAN'T SEE A THING TILL YOU OPEN MY EYES. I CAN'T SEE A THING TILL YOU OPEN MY EYES. I CAN'T SEE A THING TILL YOU OPEN MY EYES. The girl raised her bare arms in the air, her eyes and her smile pure rapture. *Be one in self-harmony,* she yelled, *and arise, great warrior, arise!...*

The process by which his historical self grew lighter and more carefree continued, through 1966 and into 1965. He was involved with the campaign to save Viola Liuzza. There were things being said, information that was being released to the press, about how Viola was a member of the Communist Party of America, about how Viola enjoyed sexual relations with African-American men despite the fact that she was married and a mother. She was a civil rights activist. That was the story. All these other things were lies and it was his job to go out into the world and scoop them up, that was his job, to scoop up all the lies. There he was talking on the telephone, scooping all the words up. There he was typing, snick-snick-snick, removing ink from letters and stories and memos that were not distributed or stored on file. He sucked them all up until there was nothing left, until Viola was just an activist who was killed by Klansmen in Wayne State. In the weeks following all his hard work dismantling the smear campaign, he was discouraged because it turned out that one of the men who had shot Viola Liuzza as she drove local marchers home in her 1963 Oldsmobile, one of the Klansmen who put a bullet in her head, worked for the FBI. One of his own men had let him down. It was terrible. But then Viola wasn't dead anymore. She was just one of many people horrified by images of the aborted march on Edmund Pettus Bridge, one of a vocal minority, but then she wasn't even that. She disappeared from his radar and he felt much better, was much happier in his work, was exonerated, felt like, as the days and the nights drew in on themselves and the winter of 1965 gave way to the autumn of 1964, happier. Happier than he'd ever been. Working alongside cryptographers as part of the VENONA decrypts, infiltrating the CPUSA, working for the good of the country against those no-good commie bastards, a hero, he was a hero again, he wasn't contaminated, life was good, he worked the side of right, was a good man, had a wife, had a future, spent evenings talking about children, worked but kept work and home life separate, *had* a home life, was happy, was a good man, was a good, happy man…

Two…

His future self was anxiously scanning the crowd for Tuck, they'd got split up, the two of them, somehow, and so he was looking, roaming, another Jagger-not-Jagger singing about *THE BANKS OF THE RIVER CHARLES, AW THAT'S WHAT'S HAPPENIN' BABY, OH THAT'S WHERE YOU'LL FIND ME, ALONG WITH THE LOVERS, THE FUGGERS AND THIEVES, AW BUT THEY'RE COOL PEOPLE.* There were gangs and clusters and cliques amid the milling patchouli throng. Young girls with ironed hair in patchwork dresses with bare legs and bare feet and beads. Hairy Raskolnikoffs with open shirts and velvet jackets and flowers. Guys in leather with greasy hair and tattoos stalking women with snake-eyes and snake-lips and snake-hips. Groovy, freakish could-be boys, could-be girls in gold and silver shirts and trousers dancing, spinning with their hands outstretched like fluttering fanatic butterflies. The light show on the stage was becoming frantic, gulls swooping, missiles flying, freaks and pigs clashing in the streets, flowering tapestries of intersecting purple and red diamonds, red and white circles and oily blobs of yellow and orange, cosmic light beams lurching drunkenly over the faces of those near by, transforming stupid, vacant-looking hippy kids into phantoms and spectres and hobgoblins, the Grande Ballroom a shabby haunted house, host to the end of the world. Vedder thought he saw silver-bearded John Sinclair pointing at him over the heads of the crowd, laughing like a demented iron fox from the future. He saw Tuck the instant the music cut, over by the fire exit, waylaid by Panthers. A short guy in a leather jacket with wild hair and sunglasses, arms outstretched like a lay preacher, advanced on the stage, the crowd roaring, a short history of white noise, people clapping, clapping, clapping. BROTHERS AND SISTERS!!! he yelled. BROTHERS AND SISTERS! I WANT TO SEE YOU, SEE YOUR HANDS OUT THERE, WANT TO SEE YOU, SEE YOUR HANDS. Tuck was trying to assert some control over the situation, had his badge out, but the Panthers, one of the Panthers at least, slapped at his hand and the badge disappeared. I WANT EVERYONE TO KICK UP SOME NOISE! I WANT TO HEAR SOME REVOLUTION OUT THERE, BROTHERS. I WANT TO HAVE A LITTLE REVOLUTION! Vedder stood there, watching Tuck as the crowd roared and jeered, shouting and screaming. BROTHERS AND SISTERS! THE TIME HAS COME FOR EACH AND EVERY ONE OF YOU TO DECIDE WHETHER YOU ARE GOING TO BE THE PROBLEM OR WHETHER YOU ARE GOING TO BE THE SOLUTION. *Thasss right*, someone close by hissed. YOU MUST CHOOSE, BROTHERS, YOU MUST CHOOSE! Vedder could feel it, what the man on the stage was saying, could feel it in his own heart and in his own chest. *Arise, great warrior,*

arise! IT TAKES FIVE SECONDS, he yelled. FIVE SECONDS
OF DECISION! FIVE SECONDS TO REALISE YOUR PURPOSE
HERE ON THE PLANET. Tuck was wheeling about, same time
as he scanned the crowd, wanting Vedder to emerge out of the
dark like the goddamned cavalry or something only he had no
intention of saving the day. He was watching. He was listening.
He was feeling it, man. IT'S TIME TO MOVE. IT'S TIME TO GET
DOWN WITH IT. BROTHERS, IT'S TIME TO TESTIFY. Someone
almost standing on his shoulder yelled, Oh yeah! *Oh yeah!*
THE DAY IS GOING TO COME WHEN WE ARE ALL GOING
TO HAVE TO TESTIFY. More people were yelling now. Yeah!
Oh yeah! I KNOW I'M READY TO TESTIFY AND I WANT TO
KNOW ARE YOU READY TO TESTIFY? THE GOLDEN ARMS OF
ZENTA ARE GOING TO REACH DOWN – he jabbed a finger into
the crowd, pointed right at Vedder, it seemed – AMONG EVERY
SINGLE ONE OF YOU AND YOU'LL HAVE TO GET DOWN AND
TESTIFY THEN! Vedder was shivering. Rooted to the spot. ARE
YOU READY? Vedder nodded. Ignoring Tuck. Tuck a million
miles away from where he was. Tuck lost. Tuck gone for ever.
People mounted the stage, men in shiny silver jackets with big
hair strapping instruments to themselves like explosives. I OFFER
TO YOU RIGHT NOW! A TESTIMONIAL!!! THE MC5!!!

Centred on Warren and Forest, his arrested self felt the heat,
the heat of the crowd and the heat of the historical self burning
with righteousness and devotion even as the petrol bomb struck
and restruck the Detroit office of the Committee to End the War
in Vietnam, fire and flame, the *whoomph* over and over again,
his historical self burning brighter and still brighter as his future
self stood transfixed, pending, on the edge, MC5 errupting,

JUNG-JUNG-JUNG-JUNG, their noise and volume like fifty electrical storms, his future self charred and burned as if sheet lightning were intersecting him at fifty different points on his body simultaneously. JUNG-JUNG-JUNG-JUNG. Within their deep infinity he saw in-gathered and bound by love in one volume the scattered leaves of all the universe. The light of a thousand suns suddenly arose in the sky. JUNG-JUNG-JUNG-JUNG. *MY LOVE IS LIKE A RAMBLING RO-OSE.* JUNG-JUNG-JUNG-JUNG. His historical self obliterating even as his future self exploded, divided and dividing, taking all the paths not taken, plunging headlong into the future even as MC5 *THE MORE YOU FEEL IT THE MORE IT GROWS* JUNG-JUNG-JUNG-JUNGED. His future self disgraced before the Citizen's Commission to Investigate the FBI. His future self disgraced before the Church Committee. His future self up to his eyes in the Keith case. And all the radicalism for nothing. No civil war. No end to the war. Not for years. War and strife and civil unrest for years, for decades, but stripped of all of its effectiveness. No winners. No believers. Just war and his part in it. *RAMBLIN' ROSE. RAMBLIN ROSE. I'M GONNA PUT YOU DOWN.* JUNG-JUNG-A-JUNG, JUNG-JUNG-A-JUNG, JUNG-JUNG-A-JUNG. The petrol bomb striking the window, blooming and flowering, blooming and flowering, even as the light show behind the band bloomed and flowered, even as the noise shook his bones, scouring him, carving him hollow even as the historical self black to calmed, the exploding exploding exploding exploding like spiders across the stars—

One...

And then, suddenly, it was so simple. Everything was laid out before him, everything that was and everything that would be.

He saw it all, he held all within him and he was, momentarily, everything. An offer was made, an offer he wanted no part of, and his refusal cancelled all that had been, nullified the diffusion, restored him once more – but he was changed and, rather than complete the arc and throw the petrol bomb at the Detroit office of the Committee to End the War in Vietnam, he stopped, paused, turned about and returned to the car, Tuck instantly crazy, asking him *whattthehellyou* – even as the rag's flame caught the bottle and the Highland-green Ford Mustang split like a cheap joke cigar.

little trouble girl

emily carter roiphe

The name Sonic Youth brings an instant jerk to my shoulders and my toes curl with revulsion... not that their music is bad, in fact I kind of like it, especially the Neil Young influenced thrash and trash guitar. It may have to do with envy of course. I was in the same town at the same time and I most emphatically did not get famous. The cameras came down to record the Spoken Word scene at the Nuyorican Café exactly three weeks after I had gone to Minnesota for chemical dependency treatment. Not only that, there was a huge riot in Tompkin's Square Park the very next day – not the Riot Grrl kind with suicidal nymphettes in house slips shouting and refusing to bow down to anyone's patriarchal definition of knowing how to 'play' an instrument, but the real kind, with cops on horseback hitting people on the skull so hard that they bled internally into their brain cavities. Horrible, but I should have been there, it was part of the history of my city. Sonic Youth was in the East Village air a lot in those days – but mostly as background noise for me and the aspiring writers with whom I came in contact. Their looks embarrassed me, frankly, by illustrating my own pretensions – sullen, arty looking white kids who were attempting to cop some sort of attitude while meanwhile there was actual poverty, tragedy and child abuse everywhere you looked, along with art, of course, on every spare square inch, art and music. I can remember them doing a sound check in the Tompkin's Square bandshell one morning, no fun for my ears, and watching a dispute going on just east of the stage. One of the many instant art collectives that banded and disbanded by the week had put up a piece of 'guerrilla' art, guerrilla because it had neither been funded nor zoned... an act of defiance. A guy from the collective – who would today be called a 'hipster' – and a woman, who looked like, but was not, Kim Gordon, were disputing with the parents of a couple of kids. The 'guerrilla' art looked like a festive and many-coloured jungle gym, and some kids were trying to climb on it. No, no, the arty guy goes, it's dangerous, stop... The woman said something about cordoning it off. One kid's father, who was drinking a tallboy, was bellowing loud and full of wounded swagger, 'The fuck you put something like that up in fuckin park, the kids can't fuckin play on it? I'll sue your ass...' One of the band's roadies or someone got on the mike and tried to calm everyone down, in the same manner and with just as much efficacy as Mick Jagger at Altamont crooning 'brothers and sisters' to a crowd of Hell's Angels on methamphetamine and PCP. The mother of some other kids started screeching that *her kid had got hurt, a bottle was hurled and the artists fled, their sunglasses falling off, carefully moussed coiffures a-wobble. The band played on... Art has no reason to consider practical things like the fact that putting up a sculpture that looks like something kids could play on but wasn't might not be the best way to contribute to the community. No time to consider that art-noise-rock-screech soundcheck might be the one bit of indifference that would send a depressed, chemically dependent college drop-out over the edge, especially when she looked at Kim Gordon, all ice-cool and swan-like aloofness while the college drop-out scraped the dirty sweat off her own forehead with a matchbook. Ah well, Sonic Youth fades, but Sonic Middle Age also has something to be said for it. I just wish I hadn't missed so much of the genuine art and music (Sonic Youth included, for all I know) that was bubbling around in the 1980s. Compulsion was yanking me around in those days, and compulsion, no matter what anyone says, is the exact opposite of rock and roll.*

||||||||||||||||||||||||||||||

The Minneapolis addiction medicine clinic's waiting room is quite small and acoustically tiled. Still, it vibrates with a faint fluorescent hum. One entire wall is taken up with a poster bearing a diagram of emphysematic lungs, which sits behind a glass case so no one can steal it. For such a small waiting area it contains a global cross-section of humanity. Sitting in little plastic chairs, waiting to dose, we often look like some kind of small-world diorama designed by Walt Disney if he'd been chronically depressed.

Aside from the African-Americans from Indiana and Chicago, there are the Native Americans whose antibuse is mixed with the pink Oral Metha-dose in their dixie cups. There are the women, white, black and native, who bring their kids in.

'He's got the croup. That's why he's not in school.'

Once I saw a mother hemming the cuffs of her nine-year-old son's suit as she waited to get her methadone. 'He's going to his first dance,' she explained.

'Are you excited?' asked a man who could have been either thirty-five or sixty. 'I'd be excited if I was going to see my first dad.'

No one informed him of the fact that he'd misheard dad for dance. A still silence settled over the room. The hard-time Midwestern white guys stared at the emphysema poster, sitting stock still in the small plastic chairs the colour of baby aspirin, the spidery lines around their eyes etching out the words: 'Her fault'.

By rights I should sit with the ageing punk rockers, those in various shades of black denim, just held together by layers of grime, soot and ash, oil and studs. They seem to have been wearing their outfits for thirty years, or since the last time they cared about 'fashion', or even 'anti-fashion'. Perhaps it took that long to create the look with any kind of authenticity. The really young ones have dreadlocks and facial tattoos, homeless kids, runaways, they mess up my mind with a split between maternal instinct and wondering where they got the money to even get an opiate dependence to begin with, especially in Minnesota, where a ten dollar bag from New York or Chicago costs fifty bucks. It can be done, of course...

but first off you have to sell or pawn your possessions and these little ones didn't look like they had any. The boys I don't know, but the little girls, while still lovely, were not exactly 'escort service' material. All these children – maybe started out in the farmland areas, babies in the big town.

It's *not* a big town, of course, not New York or Chicago; social service lines move fast so people can afford to be chatty. Still, if it wasn't for the bright splashes of Hmong community colour, I might think that all that was left in the world were shades of darker and lighter grey.

The Hmong are here at the clinic to get a small taste of an opiate, the herbal and organic version of which is no longer available to them here. In their traditional culture, the elderly would take a bit to ease the inevitable aches and pains of ageing. As in every culture, some people stray from tradition and into obsession. It seems ridiculous in a way, for them to be on methadone – opium being a much less potent drug than any kind of synthesised opiate Western medicine can offer. I do not know what kinds of problems smoking opium caused and still causes, but it can't be as hard to detox from as methodone... Can it? Or do they have to take it because it's an opiate-blocker, simply to prevent them from getting high. I am as lost thinking about their lives as they must be having landed here – a frozen, metal planet navigable only by their children.

Still, I am always so glad to see them because they have yet to 'assimilate' – or succumb to the rules of our metro-area camouflage. The women wear brightly embroidered hats and headscarves, exuberantly patterned skirts with shirts that don't match. Checks, flowers, beads, narrow stripes, wide stripes, textile mosaics – all in a single outfit, the desired effect being an approximation of the clothes they wore at home. They refuse, in other words, to abandon the beautiful for the appropriate. If you want to talk to them you have to speak either to their generally polite and sociable kids or to Wat. Wat is a counsellor and community liaison and is able to tell jokes in three languages, including, I suspect, Latin.

He thinks I am funny because I am always having trouble with my car. 'Hey...' he cajoles, when I use the front desk phone again. Once more calling my husband, Nurse Johnnie, to pick me up because my car won't start in the −20 degree Fahrenheit February temperatures: '...Always Car Trouble... You Little Red Riding Hood. Car Trouble is you wolf. Little Trouble Girl.'

I am not a young girl any more, but an actual young one pipes up next to me. 'That's a song... Little Trouble Girl...'

Leopard-print coat, died orange hair, pale white make-up over acne... Is she even twenty-five? What's she been googling? More to the black and howling point: which one of my aborted children is she...?

Wat is fascinated. '...A song?'

'Yeah, Sonic Youth,' she says. 'They were a group. They had a song that was called something like "Little Trouble Girl".'

And although I always say I'll keep quiet, I never, ever do. The memory crashes through the window, horn honking, shattered glass, headlights on high beam: how they used to warm up before they performed in Tompkin's Square Park, which was practically my front yard at the time, their snarling but somehow affectless music sending its barbed tendrils through the window of my first-floor apartment, yanking me into another day full of withdrawal, no money, desperation, guilt and a permanent taste in my mouth of having swallowed an ashtray. They were Hell's alarm clock.

I hated the sound they made, as if they were not really angry, but using the sounds and chord progressions of anger to create something that was wilfully hard to interpret. I was in the minority though, most people liked them in those days, not that anyone would have used the word 'liked'. No one ever had any expression on their faces, you had to know someone very well before you declared an actual opinion, lest you show enthusiasm. It was as if eighth grade would never end, and no one, but no one, no matter how much they supposedly knew me, would ever lend me ten dollars to try to buy something that wouldn't leave me conned and shaking, as sick as I was before. That was the sound *I* made.

'God,' I said to the youngster: 'I hated that group.'

She looked confused. If I'd been so unhip as to hate Sonic Youth how was it that I'd lived right upstairs from where they played so many of their famous gigs?

Wat, as usual, thought the whole thing was funny. 'One person's tea is other person's urine sample.'

The clinic had mostly cleared out by this time and Wat, accompanied by the little retro-punker, came outside with me to have a look at the car. She said she could possibly give it a jump. 'Thanks, sweetie.' I smiled at her. She smiled back, blushing under her clown-white foundation; two red splashes of colour it took a bit of willpower not to pinch.

In the parking lot we stood under the huge, brushed steel siding of the winter sky. This is the view of the city you get when you are by the outskirts, it's downtown still rising up before you: a scraped and lead-tinted scene of smoked-glass windows like a million sightless, square eyes, wind-crazed ribbons of white steam rising from invisible heating ducts, overpasses arcing off into the distance, shelters tucked away, where only the people who need them know how to get to the line they will have to stand on.

We gathered around my 2003 BMW – a gift from a deceased relative. 'Nice car,' Wat declared, as if to encourage me. 'Must be nice.' The young woman smiled; the expression and smile distinctly regional, a local way to express envy and suspicion while attempting to conceal.

Just then, however, I didn't like my car very well at all. In the first place I don't like cars since I didn't learn to drive until I was thirty-nine years old and never became comfortable with them. In the second, someone had clearly broken into mine. The door handle had been hit with some kind of mallet, which was entirely unnecessary since I deliberately didn't lock it in the hopes that it would be stolen and I would have an excuse to get a car that worked.

'That's new.' I nodded at the dented handle, and yanked the door towards me. At first I thought my car alarm had gone off. But then the young woman grabbed Wat's arm and pointed, stuttering. The sound *was* an alarm, of sorts, and had the same jarring effect, more so because the shriek wasn't mechanical but organic, a sharp, desperate, instantly panic-inducing wail coming from inside a tiny bundle of pink blankets.

In two years of coming to the clinic, I had seen Wat almost every day, but I had never once seen him look startled the way he was now. He even spoke in his own language first before he translated, which he never did with us English speakers.

'Oh God's dammits,' he blurted, and reached down and picked up a small bundle.

The infant squirmed faintly. Its mouth looked like the kind of rosebud you would see in a florist shop behind a refrigerated glass counter – tiny, moist and fresh, dusted with ice crystals. I didn't know where Wat had come from; I wondered whether he had seen babies before, abandoned or dead babies. God's Dammits.

I grabbed at the piece of paper pinned to the blanket. It said: 'You have nicist car at methdone clinic.'

The young punk girl stared and stared. I looked at Wat.

'OK,' he said, 'OK. Someone got confuse-d.' He hit the '*d*' on the end of confused hard, as if it didn't come naturally to him to put things in the American past tense, but he was the social worker. He would know what to do.

And what, if I looked at things realistically, did I know? The titles of certain old songs, many of which I had never liked to begin with. And the young woman? She didn't even know how old those songs really were. I held out my arms to Wat.

'For one minute,' he said, 'then we have bring her to safe release spot in ER.'

All around us things were cold, with no awnings or trees to break the blasts of wind. The baby's living body, in contrast, felt shockingly warm.

'This Little Trouble Girl,' he said. 'Not a song this time.'

He was diplomatically unclear as to which one of us he was speaking.

I held the baby for one minute. Sixty seconds is a long time to stand without talking in a windswept parking lot, looking at a baby with a rosebud mouth, a very, very little trouble girl, who is going – facts are facts – to see a lot of trouble.

on the strip

rachel trezise

*When the opportunity to contribute to Noise emerged,
I'd recently returned from a month-long trip to the
States where I was struck by the huge chasm between
the lifestyles of the rich and poor (although this seems
to be an increasing problem in the UK, too). I wanted
to write about it, but I had no idea what form the
writing would take or what kind of character(s) it
would focus on. 'On the Strip' was the ideal vehicle,
most obviously because the lyrics seem to be about a
teenage runaway trying to survive in the big city. (I
was particularly enamoured with the line 'messing
with stars and doing tricks'.) But also because the track
has two faces: Gordon's glib and sublime vocals and a
raw and grubby guitar breakdown towards the end of
the song, indicative of something dirty and unknown,
hiding behind the palpable.*

||||||||||||||||||||||||||||||||||||

Thursday night, amber sun setting in the pink sky, distant neon stuttering on. Melissa turns out of La Brea, left on Sunset. New-old black patent ballet pumps nipping the hardened skin of her toes. Love-heart tattoo on her sallow ankle, from when her body belonged to her. Ironic, actually: her ankle'd never known any stupid fucken love. Struts past people eating dinner at Clafoutis, half-plastic retards who came here on the short bus, expecting some fucken nothin'. Throws her clumsy sequin purse back on her shoulder, keeps walking. Passes a smoke shop, a fat black guy on the leather couch, staring out at her, a chunky brown cigar hiding his sneering mouth. 'Fuck you,' she says under her breath, the words never far from her lips, going around and around in her head like she has Tourette's. Probably does, has every fucken thing else. 'Fuck you. Fuck you. Fuck *you*.' That's all it's worth saying to some people. Sometimes, she wishes she had a dick so she could really fuck them; a fucken big eighteen-inch tool to bust some pussy apart. Ironic, actually.

At the liquor store, she pulls a bunch of coins out of her hot-pants; eight dollars, ten cents. The clerk watches her in the mirror as she slowly roams the aisles, the bright lights illuminating her paper-white skin, her skanky leather coat. She picks bottles up, one after another, holding them in her bitten, juddering fingers, squinting at the labels. Then she takes a quart of Grey Goose to the counter.

The clerk frowns at her.

'I ain't got no ID,' she says, grinning, revealing a broad gap where her incisor should be. She does have an ID, a fake one, in her purse someplace. She can't be bothered looking for it now.

And he sells her the vodka after all.

Back up the sidewalk, at Larrabee, a group of kids hanging out by the Viper Room, a boy and two girls gathered under the awning. 'Man, I *am* pissed at that asshole,' the guy says, kicking the fireplug, because the doorman won't let him in. Bruce Barry, cute little wild kid who peddles itsy bits of coke, PCP sometimes.

Melissa throws her purse back on her shoulder, walks towards them.

'Hey,' one of the girls says, pointing at Melissa's pantyhose. 'I just love those stockings. They're sweet.' Fucken satellite dish for a face, hybrid Brit–Yank accent; daughter of some overpaid sex-addict movie star with a condo in Brentwood. Fucken place is overrun with teenagers trying to outdo their parents, kids with credit cards for brains. They all want to hang out with 'real' people, get a taste of some authentic rebellion. Go around talking to the bums in Barnsdell Park.

Melissa looks down at the leopard-print nylon clinging to her legs. Stole them from a thrift store in Pasadena last week, still stinking of some other bitch's cunt juice. These rich kids, they love all that shit.

'Sweet,' the girl says again, nodding to herself, probably picking up CBS.

The other girl lights a cigarette, takes a long, hard drag. About the most shocking thing you can do in Hollywood, inhale nicotine. Ironic, actually.

Bruce is still kicking the hydrant, eyes as wide as cookies. Sugared off his pretty little face. Fucken kids. Find all kinds of narcotics hidden in their parents' closet but they can't order themselves a fucken Martini. Melissa unthreads her bottle top, throws it at the trash can, lifts the bag to her mouth. Bruce watches as she swallows the scorching liquid, holding the bottle-neck in her lips, sucking like a baby. He saunters up to the wall, waits for a couple of tourists to pass. Drives his hand in his pants pocket.

Melissa follows him, gives him what's left of the quart, takes the baggie out of his manicured fucken hand.

'*All* right,' he says, peering at the sticker. 'Vodka, dude.'

Melissa holds a thumbful of powder to her nostril, snorts. Stupid crumb of flake, stepped on fourteen or fifteen fucken times. Didn't care for toot after all; just a starter preceding an entrée, like a basket of fucken bread.

West again, towards the end of the strip, throwing her purse on her shoulder, muscles anaesthetised a little. Involuntary tears in her eyes, the store signs blurring into calligraphy, coloured lights reflecting in the patent of her shoes. Stops next to the big Hustler depot, stands in the darkness on Beverly Drive. 'Relax… It's Just Sex,' it says, on the customers' paper bags. Stupid rich sluts and amateur porn actresses, coming and going, armfuls of toys and DVDs, tossing their useless money into the savings account of a paraplegic, someone who is incapable of having sex. As if a fucken big rubber dildo *liberates* them. She shifts her weight from one foot to the other, pushing the blow around her system, an itsy buzz at the top of her spine. Back on the Strip. The best money in the whole of the state. She doesn't come here too often, though. Doesn't go anywhere too often. Keep moving around, otherwise people get to recognising you. The other trick is, only do white guys. Get caught up with anyone from South Central, you've already slit your own fucken throat. No colours, no blacks, no Meskins, no Gooks. Then you might be all right. Those motherfuckers talk to each other, live in tight little communities. Caucasians don't even look at each other; they hate the fucken sight of themselves. Rattle on about how much their stretch Hummer cost, wouldn't say nothing 'bout no hooker case it got back to their butt-ugly wife.

Half hour later *the* car rolls up. Ratty-looking guy in an olive Honda Accord, eyes set too close together. He stares out of the windshield, all cautious and jumpy. Melissa pouts at him, sizing him up as she slowly folds back a lapel, revealing what's on offer. Mr John Doe: average white American with two kids in elementary school, and a wife who don't give head. She gets in the car, sets her purse on her scrawny knees. He turns left, drives vigilantly along the Strip, past the groups of kids outside the Roxy, trying to sell tickets for tonight's show. Past the lit signpost at the Rainbow Bar & Grill. 'So what's the damage, honey?' he says, as he signals on to Doheny. 'For the works, the whole thing?'

Melissa shrugs. Grins an itsy bit. Make them think it's your first time doing this sort of thing, then you're halfway there. 'Two hundred dollars?' she says, all practised hesitance. Looks up at him with puppy-dog peepers. *Damage.* He got that right.

'One fifty?' he says, acting the operator. Corduroy fucken pants, the chicken-flavoured top ramen he ate for dinner still on his breath. He's pulling into an empty car lot behind Greystone Park. The headlights cut two parallel streaks through the darkness, illuminating the thick laurel bush surrounding the lot, a pile of trash and a ripped couch in one corner. He twists the key, the engine ticking down. The lights disappear. He looks at her, one eyebrow raised.

Unhooks her seat belt, that's the first thing Melissa does. 'Show it to me,' she says. 'Show me the cash.' Quickly she unties the ribbons holding her purse together, while he gropes around in his pants. Swiftly circumvents the thin lining of the purse, feeling for the A-shaped handle. She's got its nickel contour in her hand when the guy turns back to her, a bunch of twenty-dollar bills rolled up in a rubber band, balancing in his fleshy palm. He puts it on the dash, smiling proudly, the red light from the digital clock reflecting in the white of his right eye. 'Protection?' Melissa says. 'You got that?' He releases a high-pitched, swooshy little giggle, as if to say, *Of course I've got that*, starts scrabbling about in his frayed pants again. Melissa whips the butterfly knife from her purse, sticks him in his thigh.

'Haaar,' the guy yells, jerking back in his seat, his hand going to the leg, a plastic condom wrapper diving from his fingers. His itsy, screwy eyes popping from their sockets like eggs from a hen's snatch.

Melissa sits up on the bucket seat, pounds his groin with her clenched fist. Paralyses him for a moment while she stretches over his reeling body, releases the driver's door. 'Come on, asshole,' she says, 'get out.' Shoves him. Elbows him. He drops on to the ground, his frame warped into a malformed fetal position, one leg sprawled under the car, bawling like a kid. 'What is this?' he's saying, words jammed with drool. Melissa crawls into the driver's seat. Thrusts one leg out the door, lands a ballet pump on his chest, holds him still while she heaves the blade out of his leg. 'What is this?' he hollers, rolling around in the dirt.

'It's a fucken carjack, you asshole,' she says. She throws her blade under the passenger seat, starts the engine, slams the door. Runs over something, probably his foot, says, 'Fuck you, fuck you, fuck…' Licentious men are so weak and stupid. They'd turn themselves inside out looking for a spanking-wet pussy; wouldn't see no danger comin' till it'd slit their fucken throats. *Don't worry about him.* He's not gonna die. He's not gonna go to the rollers either, 'cause they'd bust him for soliciting. Don't you know? Prostitutes go to heaven. It's their clients that go to hell.

The money roll falls into her lap as she turns back on to Sunset. *Damage. Protection.* Ironic, actually.

It wasn't always this fucken easy. She wasn't always this fucken astute. When she first came to California, as green as the shit in a discarded diaper, she hung around with a couple other girls, on Los Feliz and Vermont. One night, four years ago, a gleaming black Aston Martin with Florida licence plates pulled up against the sidewalk. This hand came out of the electric window, thick, clean fingers gesturing at her. She couldn't believe that he chose *her*. The other girls were from the Valley, wore vinyl miniskirts and heavy gold hoop earrings. They'd stand a little away from the edge, legs crossed at the knee, their fists planted on their big butts, bangles from their wrists to their elbows. Their pimps taught them all that shit: what to wear, how to act, they'd been doing it for years. Melissa had only done it once. She could still taste the burnt-rubber tang on her tongue, from giving some fucken rich medical freshman a blowjob two days before. 'Just close your eyes,' Stephanie'd said, slurring. 'You won't even feel it. You won't feel a thing.' That bitch must have turned all her tricks high as a fucken moose, 'cause when you lose one sense, the other four get stronger.

The john was an old Dago, leather rhinoceros skin. His car smelt like high-priced cologne. Melissa liked riding in that car. The stereo was playing classical music, all piano and violin, real fucken dramatic and all. He turned the volume low, to ask her name.

'Melly,' she said, because that's what those bitches called her. Then she said, 'That's short for Melissa, sir,' thinking she owed him some kind of fucken explanation.

'How old are you, Melissa?' he said, in his soft, mangled, Italian accent. 'Fourteen, sir,' she said.

He smiled, his thin, purple lips stretching over flawless white veneers. She remembered those teeth. She'd blocked the rest of his sleazy fucken face out of her memory, but those perfect Disneyworld gnashers, they were there. The red leather seats were covered in thin plastic sheets. She asked him why, just for something to say. She didn't know what else to fucken say. She'd never met anyone with a car that neat. Hell, the Governor of Oregon didn't have a car like that. He said it'd just come back from the valet. He drove to a hill on the other side of the Hollywood Freeway. 'Is this good?' he said. Melissa giggled, directed him farther along the dirt track, away from an alleyway with a security bulb. A guy like that, she expected good money. The last thing she wanted was to get busted. Jennifer had been bitching all week, about how quiet it was, too fucken quiet, how she was getting sick. She had some herb but it wasn't what she needed. Melissa figured she'd have enough left over to buy her a bit of junk. She was *that* fucken naive. Those hizzies knew what was going down. If they didn't, they would have got in that fucken car themselves.

But that was then, and Melissa was about as sharp as a fucken coconut, still blinded by the sunshine and the fucken palm trees. As he drove slowly across the gravel, she thought about how one day she'd have a car like this, and clothes and jewellery, how she'd smell like the fragrance counter in Rite Aid. How she could make it up with her Aunt Maria back in Portland, make her understand that she hadn't been lying about what Uncle Larry had done to her. They could go to the mall together, buy home wares from Saks. Maybe this guy would fall in love with her, become a regular. Maybe he'd set her up in her own little place out in Malibu. Man, she was fucken whack.

She felt a hard slap across her cheek and noticed the car had stopped. She reached to unbuckle her belt, but too quickly he slammed her square in the face, broke her nose. She felt it deflate, depress into her head. Her throat filled with a rush of gluey liquid, the rusty tang of blood. She held her seat for balance, trying to stop her head hitting the window, the dashboard, her fingernails cutting into the plastic. If she was yelling she couldn't hear herself. He found a spot that really hurt; a hollow gully between her earlobe and her jaw. He kept beating on that, again and again and again, until Melissa lost consciousness. It took about thirty minutes. She doesn't know what happened after that. But the nurse said later that they found semen residue in her ear canals.

She woke up dead, almost, a day or so later. Lying inside a dumpster, slouched against its aluminium wall, her head stooped on her chest. Somehow, she managed to sit up, kneeled on a ripped garbage sack, pushed the roof open. The sunlight burnt her eyes. She limped to the intersection, stomach bowed, trying to avoid the shingle on the ground. She was barefoot. Couldn't remember what shoes she'd had on. Figured she was in Westwood, from the signboard for the San Diego Freeway, a couple of girls in rollerblades. She tried to hitch a ride but those motherfuckers wouldn't stop. She swore she saw a patrol car that ignored her. Somewhere along the sidewalk she caught sight of herself in the plate-glass window of a gas station, realised why. Her face was just one big fucken wound;

a head like a fucken hole. Part of it had scabbed. She tried to swipe her tongue out of her lips, to wash some blood away. But her mouth wouldn't work. Globs of American cheese clinging to her ripped dress, an onion sliver, blood and hamburger relish. It took her two hours to get to the Cedars Sinai Medical Centre.

But she was never that fucken dumb again. Started working stuff out pretty quick. Saw the city looking like what it was: a fucken crack-whore house. Hiding behind those palm trees, underneath the stars on the Walk of Fame, everything that isn't glamorous: fucken homicidal Mafia minions who like ejaculating in little babies' smashed-up faces. And worse. Ironic, actually. And to live somewhere like that, to stay alive, you gotta think like a fucken crack whore.

On the opposite end of the Strip, across the street from the yellow train car restaurant, she sees a pusher she's dealt with before. A fat guy with a red beard, hiding in the shadows behind the Body Shop. She turns north on Sweetzer, flips around, pulls up right next to him. 'Hey,' she says, summoning him. He takes a quick look around, at a UCLA student leaving Wal-Mart with a case of soda, at the billionaires' dumb kids, lined up in their turbo Nissans, heading to nightclubs, peroxide updos that cost more than one-bed apartments. The dealer walks to the car, scooches down at the window.

'Dope?' Melissa says, the bills in her hand. It's all she has to fucken say.

'Yeah, baby,' he says.

She drives away with the smack on the seat between her legs, towards the hills via Selma, past the Chateau Marmont where

Belushi said *goodnight*. That's all Hollywood is about: death. Charlie Manson drawing cartoon pigs on the wall with the blood of a movie director's wife; Marilyn Monroe lying naked and self-pitying, a bottle of sedatives the only sympathy she ever got; Fitzgerald's heart packing in while he bought a packet of cigarettes in Schwab's; Peg Entwhistle throwing herself from the top of the big white H; an AIDS epidemic in Porno Valley. River fucken Phoenix. Phil fucken Spector. It ain't about bright lights, this. It's about bright lights burning out. People come here searching for a heightened experience of life; glamour and fucken sparkle, but there ain't no such fucken thing. Money can't combat it. Success don't beat it. When you get bored of living, there's only one thing left to do, and they all come to La La Land to do it, whether they know it or not. On a warm night, like tonight, you can smell the mortality, like garbage left in the sun for a week. Stewing in its own rot. It's ironic, actually.

She parks next to a culvert leading away from the Franklin reservoir, way up between Mulholland and Studio where it's dark as hell. She can barely see the sickly glow of Downtown or hear the shrieking of the freeway. She finds the butterfly knife, wipes it in her chiffon scarf. Hitches her purse over her shoulder. She leaves the car door wide open, wanders over to a navy patch of wild vegetation, sits down in a bunch of sorghum grass. She toys what's left of the blow from her hot-pants, snorts it right out of the furrowed plastic. Then she unwinds the bloodstained scarf, feels around for her shooter, unwraps her new fix. Lifting her forearm into the air, tightening the tourniquet, she sees the cigarette burns dotted along the pallid skin on her radius, and on the other side track marks the length of her ulna, clear in the moonlight, like pop-rivets holding her together. The smack kicks in, mollifies her nerves. She falls back on the ground, the grass stalks collapsing beneath her, her crossed legs flopping open. She feels her throbbing muscles thawing into liquid, her whole body melting and flowing away, dripping down into the earth, until it's all gone, until she can touch herself and not feel anything at all. No bones, no disease, no wounds, just a fucken spirit.

She did this every day, hustled her carcass only in order to free herself from it. Fucken ironic, actually. Those organs and muscles were new, eighteen years old, and yet old, fucken ironic. Perhaps one day she'd OD and she could leave the body there, on the grass, inside the dumpster, the husk, the crust which used to be her. Like one of those big-shot movie stars. But the corpse'd be anything but pretty. And it wouldn't make the E! Channel news.

rain on tin

jess walter

*Sonic Youth? Wow. Where do I start? Well, I was high
a lot, that's what I remember from those days. My own
band, PissStain, had just broken up for the fourth time
and I spent most of my time studying for my M-CATS.
In March, I was hit by a rickshaw.*

*It was right around that time I began collecting
scat from urban animals. From the apartment below
I often heard the sound of someone using a hot glue
gun. Things were unsettled. Then, some time after our
annual Arbour Day party, when the coke spoons were
melted back into fireplace tools, I moved out.*

*Anyway, after that, the inevitable drift was
inevitable. I never saw the members of Sonic Youth
again. In fact, I can't say for sure that I ever saw them
in the first place, that I remember the band or that I've
ever heard their music. I do know the Seattle Sonics.
I saw them play in an exhibition game once. And I
know of the Hitler Youth. I'm assuming Sonic Youth is
somewhere in the middle. You know, aesthetically.*

A Note for Professor Rucker:

Just so you know, there will be no sex in this story. All semester I've watched the stories the other students churn out, with all the sucking and poking and the endings that don't seem to mean a goddam thing. What is this, porno? And the way you encourage them! If it's not sex then it's drugs. And symbolism. (I still don't think you've adequately answered my question, why someone can't just write a story that's a story. And yes, I hear the skittering from the younger students, but goddam it, it's a valid question.) That's the kind of story this story is – a real story about what real people do in their real lives, and a real old-fashioned hero, whose name is Dave Burns. And no symbolism. I get so sick of all the symbolism. Why can't a tree just be a goddam tree? In this story you can bet that if there are trees they will just be trees. Not trees representing penises or pudenda. You probably are saying to yourself, oh here's old John dooming himself to another story that will never be published. Well, if that's the case, then so be it.

I assume from your enthusiasm for all the symbolism and drugs and porno in the work of the younger students that it must be all the rage in the glossy magazines to feature stories with symbols and female ejaculate and threesomes and fivesomes and multi-hour drug-enhanced engorgements. Words like pudenda.

Well, you'll find none of that here! Not that the people in this story are boring or unattractive or non-sexual, they just don't have to go on about being obsessed with putting their things where they don't belong. They're what used to be called 'adults'. Oh, you'd probably give me an A if I told that other kind of story and, trust me, I was married for twenty-six years so I know a thing or three about what people do behind closed doors. I'll bet if you just add up the sex, I've done it a lot more than those other students who go on and on about it! But if you're waiting for some description of what Connie and I did, think again. What happens between two people who love each other is sacred. I'd as soon describe the day I came home to find her naked and bled out, slumped over the tub like a goddam bathrobe, as tell you about what we did behind closed doors. Did it ever occur to you that's why people close doors?!?

So if the only point in reading short stories these sad days is the hope of being titillated by this new description of ejaculation or that new coital position then I guess this old bird is just doomed to fail. (And happy to do it!) But just this once I'd like you to put away all those preconceived ideas of 'conflict' and 'narrative architecture' and 'character construction' and Flannery O'Connor and Raymond Carver (who, I'm sorry, was a terrible writer, God-awful! Would someone tell me what happens at the end of those pitiful 'stories', and I use the word loosely) and just read this story like a goddam story, the kind of story that real storytellers used to tell, before it all became sex and drugs and liberal teachers (I'm sorry to bring politics into this, but I've seen the bumper stickers on your car. Legalise marijuana? Please!). Maybe you get more money from the university or get some kind of award in your little leftist teaching organisation if your students publish symbolism-filled sex stories in the flesh mags, or in anthologies, or get a story collection with a stylish cover showing a thigh, perhaps, or a filled ashtray, or a shirtless man on a motel bed with his head in his hands, lit through the window by the red 'Vacancy' sign of the motel.

Not that I am against being anthologised.

But this is not that sort of story.

In this story, there is simply Dave and he's just a good guy. Not complicated. An American. The good kind, no hyphens or dark past, just what used to be called a man. Late fifties but people often mistake him for someone in his early fifties. Worked in sales for years but everyone always said he was a great storyteller and he always knew he had a way with the words. Then his wife passed away of a brain tumour in Victorville (a couple of years before the story starts) and one day he just decided to go to college and he moved to Irvine and that's where the story starts, with him in college, taking undergraduate classes in various disciplines and feeling alive for the first time in years, but also feeling more like an outsider than he thought was possible. He's the oldest student by far, and people don't respect his life-knowledge and the courage it took for him to go to college. In fact, they are openly dismissive of him. He ignores their scorn because what else is he going to do, and so they become bolder in it and he ignores it more and on and on it goes, until they pretty much are laughing in his face. And yet he soldiers on, like someone in a foreign country. So that's the set-up of the story. It's a love story, which I'm sure you'll hate too.

And I know what you're thinking, but for one thing I was never in sales. I worked the warehouse in tool-and-dye, mostly assistant managing, and even though I never took a single business class, I could run circles around those college graduates they hired as purchasing agents and general managers and I outlasted all of them! So it's ironic that here I am in college. There are plenty of other differences between me and Dave too, the biggest being that my wife didn't die of a brain tumour, although I'll argue to my own death that the depression was caused by one, despite what Connie's note said about 'emptiness' and 'suffocation,' not to mention whatever psychobabble that therapist has planted in our daughter Libby about me stifling them both. Sometimes life is just hard, OK? That's what your stupid students, with their ecstasy and their little sex stories full of ironic quips to adults, don't understand. They all blame their parents for their miserable little lives, but you know what? Nobody makes your life miserable. Life makes your life miserable.

And even if Dave does have a few exterior details in common with me, you don't seem to criticise any of the other students for writing about themselves, like that black-haired girl with the tattoos who wrote the disgusting thing about giving a blowjob to her PE teacher in high school, the story you loved so much – hmm, wonder what that's about. If you don't mind a word of advice from someone who's been around some blocks, you should be careful.

Another thing about this story. In the middle part, where Dave decides he's fond of the graceful, fortyish woman who works at the sandwich shop on campus and tries to figure out how to talk to her, they say the kinds of real things that real people say to one another ('Hi.' 'How are you?' 'Nice weather we're having.') and not the senseless and overly symbolic crap that you praise as dialogue in your class. ('The ground holds its moisture better than it once did.' 'I hear the salmon have returned.' 'Lonely is easy on the weekends.') So you better not hold that against me either.

Not that my characters don't feel things deeply, but they do what people do with thoughts like those: they think them; they don't run around speaking in some literary code just to sound smart for the judges in some corrupt fiction contest sponsored by one of those writer's trade journals in which perfectly good stories are form-rejected as being 'ultimately not for us'.

noise

No, the people in this story do what people do. They get up. They watch TV. They go to class. They're lonely, but they don't go around being degenerates because of it. And if they sometimes imagine themselves with a woman and indulge in… self-pleasure, I'm not going to go on about it (pressed against the mirror, eyes squinting) like the kid with the goatee who wrote four pages about fondling himself like a monkey… and who – I'm sorry, Professor Rucker – is not the genius you seem to think he is. Please tell me where his story about beating off goes because I read it three times and it seems to me that the thing just ends. You don't even find out whether it's the babysitter outside his door or his mother or who! And he doesn't even finish… you know. That's not a story. And yet here you always go, thinking he's Hemingway or some goddam thing. We notice which students you favour, too. You should know that. And this isn't just about me, because you've made it perfectly clear that you don't think I'm going to be making any money any time soon as a writer. I know you think I'm a no-talent, argumentative old cuss, but here's a question for you, sir: why should the talented people be the only ones who get to write books?

Besides, I'm not that much older than you, and those girls in the back row might look at you a certain way now but you are fading away, right before their eyes, and you don't even know it. That's what someone my age could tell you, if you'd listen, how the girls see you, and then one day they don't any more, and how one day there's a part of you that's just living in your memories. And the older the memory, the more clear it seems to be. How after a while, when you close your eyes, you won't even be able to see your wife any more. Not her face, anyway, just her white arms streaked with drying blood and her folded back and the dark red seams of the tile you laid together in the bathroom – tile that she picked out! How's that for stifling and suffocating?

And when you do search your memory on those times you're... self-pleasing, it's not even about sex. It's about this brown-haired girl from the summer you were a camp counsellor when you were fifteen, the year your parents went to Alaska to see your uncle and you were so homesick until you met this brown-haired counsellor, a year older than you, and freckled, and it was pouring rain and the campers were all in the lodge getting a lecture about ticks and this girl – whose name you can't even remember (God, what would these kids know about an ache like that... an old man mumbling names to himself, hoping he'll come across it) – she put her hand on your lap, on the outside of your camp shorts, and just that little pressure was enough, and just the thought of that pressure now and the sound of a rainstorm one morning brings back the memory of those drops popping away on the tin roof of the dormitory and that girl's hand on your lap and the feeling that you would grow and grow and grow under her hand forever, that the world couldn't stop you from growing under that girl's hand.

But that's not what this story is about. Because I know what you'd say about that if I did write that story, about an old man – a good man – a man everyone blames for his wife's death, even though she did it her goddam self, without a bit of warning! This good man who can't even picture his wife any more and can only seem to think about this freckled girl from camp – obsess about her, almost – that it's 'sentimental', which is a word you keep using like it's negative, but you know what? I don't mind being sentimental. I'm happy to be sentimental. On my best days, the ones that are bearable anyway, I am exactly sentimental. Don't you see that it's a kind of gift to be able to find sentiment in life? I am at the end of things and the students are at the beginning and so I don't blame them, but you are somewhere in the middle and here you are with your Legalise Marijuana and your longish hair and your hands always in your pockets and your long pauses… and goddam it, you should know better! You should know that you wake up and you pray for a little sentimentality on those days when it feels black and empty and you wonder whether you've missed your whole life. You should know that but you don't. You think you know everything, but you don't know anything.

No, I know what you're going to think of this story. Too corny, too small, nothing happens. You're especially going to hate the part where the widower Dave gets up the strength to talk to the sandwich woman and she thinks he seems like a decent guy. You'll say you don't believe it, that she wouldn't go for a 'decent' guy, that there has to be something more to her attraction, but maybe sometimes that's all people want, someone to be decent to them. And maybe that's all some people have to offer. I know you're going to say something like, 'We need more about the dead wife,' but did it ever occur to you that there is no more? That people die and they're dead and that's that?

So give me a C. I don't care. The story is just going to be a story and not a druggy anatomy lesson. Dave's going to ask the brown-haired sandwich woman to go for a walk and in the end, they're going to hold hands and run to get out of the rain in a little tin-roofed gazebo that I'm putting where there is no gazebo and you can think it's corny or 'sentimental' if you want, but that's what I want to happen, goddam it. I'm not going to have her make up some excuse why she can't, and have him go back to his apartment and please himself, even if you think that's more 'believable'. He's going to say something that he's planned out, something clever and funny to the girl about the club sandwich and joining her club (you've made it abundantly clear that you don't like puns, but did you ever think that maybe she does) and she's going to agree to go for a walk and that's that. And if you can't make a little thing like that happen – a goddam walk between two people, it's not like he was asking her to marry him – if you can't make even that happen in a story, then I don't see why you'd bother writing a story at all! I don't know why you'd even bother getting out of bed in the morning, to tell you the truth.

And, in the workshop, if you urge me to continue the story, Dave and the sandwich woman kissing under a tree, their hands groping all over one another leading to we both know what... and don't think I haven't thought of that, a lot... goddam it, you're just going to have to find another student to do your dirty work. I'm not going to write a sex scene just so you can feel like you've done your job. I would rather die never having published a thing than ruin the moment by having them do anything but hold hands. Dave staring at the freckles on the sandwich lady's face. Rain falling around them.

sunday

hiag akmakjian

There's something about the song 'Sunday' that is evocative of my childhood (these things are always so personal) and the years when I was growing up. It took me back and I found myself reliving some of its happy-sad moments. A beautiful song.

||||||||||||||||||||||||||||||||||

Sunday comes alone again.

I was late for lunch. As I was leaving to go over to the Sforzas a few doors down from me, I got the call I had been expecting from the *Journal* about the photo story on Hoboken that they had proposed. The editor brought up an intricate point about secondary rights and, by the time we hung up, I was very late. Even so, old man Sforza beamed as I walked in. He was always a very affectionate and cordial man.

'Come on,' he said, 'let's get started. Everybody must be starved. Do I hear any objections?'

'No objections here,' his wife said. She was wearing her

robin's-egg-blue apron and her hair was done up in a bun behind her head.

I handed over the antipasto I had brought over, a special prosciutto I get on Ninth Avenue in Manhattan whenever I happen to be in that part of town.

Mrs Sforza yelled happily, 'No Frills – All Thrills.' That was the motto stitched on her apron which one of her sons, Dom or Paul, had given her on her birthday. She put the prosciutto on a plate with slices of honeydew melon she brought out from the fridge.

It was a very summery fall and we ate at the table in the backyard outside the ground-floor kitchen. The yard was nothing more than a cement rectangle behind the row of buildings. Individual yards were divided off by low fences of unpainted planks running from the buildings to the back alley behind the houses. There were plants in pots outside the kitchen windows, and at the back end of the Sforzas' yard was their old pear tree. It was gaunt looking and had been there since my childhood. I could see how the whole back area had a desolate look but not to the people who lived there. To us it was just a nice quiet spot in Hoboken. We didn't really see it any more.

'Good prosciutt' – the real thing,' Mr Sforza said. 'Probably from Manziano's, am I right?'

'Prosciutt'. Italians really understand ham,' Mrs Sforza said with feeling.

When we were finished with the antipasto, Mr Sforza went inside and brought out the main dish. He himself had prepared it. He enjoyed cooking what he called nuts-and-bolts food: roasts, cutlets, steaks.

'Anybody here hate capon?' he asked with a grin.

He set the platter of roasted bird at his place on the table and inhaled its aroma.

'This's going to be good,' his wife said happily.

He put three generous pieces on three plates and next to each portion added a white mound of mashed potatoes. With the ladle he poked a crater into the centres and ladled in gravy, then carefully added a large spoonful of peas alongside.

'There's plenty of gravy, so help yourself.'

He poured Chianti from a straw-covered bottle.

'*Salut*'!'

'Did you know that Hoboken is now the most densely populated city in the United States?' Mr Sforza said. 'Very few people know that. When my grandparents first arrived here back in the 1920s Hoboken was mostly empty lots with a few scattered houses. It was New York's seaport then. In fact, even when I was a kid, just before the second war, it still had that empty look. Remember?' he asked his wife. 'Not too many houses.'

Mrs Sforza nodded. 'Frankie Sinatra was around then too. Old Blue Eyes. He lived just a few blocks from here, before he became a movie star. They used to call him Frankie. Then he became Francis.'

'Old Blue Eyes,' I said. 'Probably if he had been born and raised in London, they would have made him Sir Francis.'

'In Italy,' Mr Sforza said, 'they would have made him Saint Francis.'

'They already have a Saint Francis,' Mrs Sforza said. 'Besides, Old Blue Eyes is still Frankie to me.'

She winced and eased dentures from her mouth and slid them back in again – a flash of white-and-pink upper plate. She smiled shyly when she saw me noticing.

The Castellanos – my family – and the Sforzas had been living next door to each other in Hoboken for so many years that we were more like uncles, aunts and cousins than neighbours. After my parents died, whenever I called up Mr and Mrs Sforza to ask whether I could come by and have lunch with them, always on a Sunday, they always said sure, come on over. They were much older than me and had grandchildren already but the generation gap didn't bother them and it didn't bother me – I doubt that we even thought about it. I knew they missed their sons Dom and Paul, who had been my friends as we were growing up and who had married and moved away and had families of their own. I visited Mr and Mrs Sforza out of habit but also I was aware, living next door to them, how alone they were most of the time. The sons and their wives and children visited as often as they could, but that was seldom more than once a year – but they never missed Christmas.

I liked Mr Sforza for the way he loved his wife. He was not at all sentimental. 'You have a good wife,' I once heard a friend say to him, and Mr Sforza said, 'She's OK.' 'Just OK?' '*Very* OK.' He confided to me later, in case I might wonder whether there was some secret to his marital happiness, 'She's a woman you have to adjust to.' I said that made her sound difficult and I hoped he didn't mean it that way, and he laughed as though I were cracking some dumb kind of joke and said: 'No, no, no, she's easy. It's an *easy* adjustment.' Which left me in the dark. 'In other words, she's OK,' I said as a prompt, hoping he would build on that and say something different. '*Very* OK,' he replied in complete agreement.

I liked Mrs Sforza even more – a lot of quiet energy packed into that small aproned frame and old-world look. The way her soft white hair was drawn to a tight bun behind her head gave her a daguerreotype look: 'Peasant Woman, Abruzzi 1850'. I liked her eyebrows too – bushy and pure white, rising and falling almost comically. As she listened intently to what you said they would slide up and down with interest.

The Sforzas usually asked for family news and I always went prepared. I told them about my mother's oldest niece, Lucy, who had married a college traveller for Prentice-Hall because, she said seriously, he was gone most of the time and she liked the quiet. We all knew her husband and knew what she meant.

'Ralph, Lucy's youngest son. Remember him? He just got accepted at Stevens.'

'Little Ralphie?' Mrs Sforza said. 'Jesus.'

'Is his health any better now?' Mr Sforza asked.

'His health has always been fine,' Mrs Sforza said. 'What does health have to do with it?'

'You're right,' he said, 'I was thinking of Angela's kid, with the lung.'

I told Mr Sforza I thought the capon was excellent and he told me I was obviously a gumba to appreciate down-home cooking.

'Old-country down-home cooking.'

Also this was no supermarket capon, he said. He got this beauty at Keller's farm, up near Lake Hopatcong.

'You went to Keller's?' Mrs Sforza asked.

'How do you think this thing got here – UPS?'

'You went back to Keller's after that remark about Italians?' Mrs Sforza said in shock.

'Oh, that was just his humour. The Kellers are nice people, believe me.'

'*Hu*-mour?' Mrs Sforza turned to me. 'He said, "Italians are good decent folk – *both* of you."'

Her husband laughed. 'Get it? That's funny.'

'I don't care about the humour part. It's the other part I don't like,' Mrs Sforza said. 'Good decent *folk*? – you kidding? *Folk*? What are we, in an operetta or something? When was the last time *his* country had a Renaissance?'

'Ah, you don't get the point. Here, have some more peas. And let me give you some more potatoes.'

Docilely she held out her plate and accepted the potatoes. I marvelled at how much she could put away for her size. She set the plate down in front of her and, rubbing her knuckles against her cheek, massaged her gums from the outside.

'I'm glad you come around once in a while,' she said. 'We eat good all the time, but we usually eat better when you're here – you know, pig out when there's company. When you're retired you pig out a lot.'

'Eating is the hobby of old age,' Mr Sforza agreed.

'In Florida, in old age, they play shuffleboard. Up here, we pig out,' his wife said.

'Down there they pig out too, don't kid yourself.'

'On frozen orange juice.'

Mr Sforza said he and his wife enjoyed our get-togethers, and he thought that one of the reasons I had been coming over more frequently in recent months was that I was unconsciously searching for my dead father.

Mrs Sforza looked aghast. 'Jesus, Marco, where were you raised? On a raft?'

My father had been a widower for a few years and then had died six months ago, of stomach cancer.

'No, hey!' Mr Sforza said to me earnestly. 'I don't mean that's the only reason you come over.' He was careful not to mention my being single now – a new thing. 'And no disrespect. It's just that you're also looking for your father. You know how horses go back to the places they used to go around to with their masters. Well, you know... people... I mean, we're not that different.'

'Jesus,' Mrs Sforza said.

'Aaah, Mike's not taking it the wrong way. He understands.'

His wife glanced over to make sure, then looking at her husband she pointed a finger at her temple and spun it round and round.

Mr Sforza continued: 'And soon we'll be gone too – the last connection with your father. Look,' he said before his wife reacted, 'I'm only saying what's true. That's the way life goes. Did I ever tell you about the time your father attempted suicide?'

Mrs Sforza slapped her hand on the table and spun away. 'Jee-zus!' She said it to her husband but she was looking at me. 'We invite the guy over for lunch and you—'

'Waidda minute, waidda minute,' Mr Sforza said. He was unflappable. 'That's what they *thought*. He would never commit suicide, your father.'

'Who's "they"?' I asked.

'The police that arrived at the scene.'

A laugh exploded from Mrs Sforza. 'Oh, *that* time!' She looked happy again.

'You serious?' I asked.

'If you mean is it a true story, yes. Your father was driving to Newark early one Sunday morning – you know, one of those days when you hardly see a car on the Pulaski Skyway. It must have been about six in the morning and it was summertime and beautiful out and he was crossing the Hackensack river when he got this sudden urge to stop at the edge of the roadway – just park the car and get out. There was nothing but empty highway as far as he could see in either direction and he figured it was safe, so he did. He leaned over the railing and looked down at the river.'

'This is good,' Mrs Sforza said to me. 'You're going to like this.' She was looking very happy now.

'Usually you hardly ever see a patrol car, especially on a Sunday morning and especially that early in the morning. But wouldn't you know it, just at that moment some state troopers or something come by and stop and one of them goes over to see if your father's OK and your father says, sure I'm OK, I was just admiring the view. The cop looks at him thinking he's maybe a little crazy or something and says he'd better go admire it someplace else and never try parking in the middle of a highway again. The cop said because there was no traffic he'd let him go this time. 'No problem,' your father said, but he just stood there hoping they'd go away so he could take another look at the river. So the trooper says, 'C'mon, c'mon, first you go, *then* we leave. I don't want no suicide on my hands.' So your father laughs. 'No, no,' he says. 'I'm a happy man. I'm enjoying life.' That's the way your father talked – the way people from Campobass' talk. We don't waste words.'

'He wasn't from Campobass',' Mrs Sforza said. 'He was Calabres'.'

'He wasn't from Campobass' but he had a cousin or something from Campobass' on his mother's side. So anyway, they all got in their cars and took off. Your father said the Hackensack looked really very beautiful from way up there.'

'Yeah, look at it from ground level some time,' Mrs Sforza said. 'Especially Jersey City. *Jee*-zus.'

Mr Sforza filled our glasses and said he knew it sounded crazy but nowadays he felt happiest with the memories of dead friends. Like my father.

'Which is not surprising. When you get to be our age, practically the only friends you have left are dead.' He said he sometimes wished he was a believer so he could say prayers for certain people, but if you don't believe, you don't believe. 'And at seventy-four you don't get converted too easy. Clara here gave up on me long ago. She told me I'm going straight to hell and not to bother to pass Go and collect my two hundred dollars. Which makes me laugh.'

'Why?'

'Well, I mean, she would be absolutely right except that there's no such place as hell. But try to tell *her* that.'

'There's no proof,' Mrs Sforza said. 'You got proof?'

'Nobody believes in hell any more.' I was attempting a little diplomacy. 'A lot of people still believe in heaven, though. Funny.'

'Heaven!' he said with a laugh. 'Right *here* is heaven. See that pear tree over there? *That's* heaven. This *lunch* is heaven and so is this wine. Here, let's have the rest of this heaven. *Salut*'!'

He poured what was left in the bottle, a little for each of us. I looked over at the spindly pear tree straining up from the cement. I had always seen the tree but had never really looked at it. It was a grouping of withered branches but it had six plump pears: there were so few leaves left you could see them all just hanging there. Compared to the tree, the pears looked young and healthy, almost gaudy, like Christmas tree ornaments. They were big and round and handsome, each one emerald green with one pink cheek, like a *Gourmet* photo spread on the beauty of orchard fruits.

Mrs Sforza saw where I was looking and said: 'They're crisp to bite into, not like those mushy yellow things you get in the supermarket. Of course, with these teeth...'

'I'll bring one over when they're ripe,' Mr Sforza said. 'You don't pick them. You wait for them to fall because that's when they have the most taste. But sometimes I help them fall. You give them a tap and see if they drop. This bunch doesn't have far to go.'

He got a long bamboo pole that had been leaning against the house, walked over to the pear tree and prodded through the scrawny branches. With the tip of the pole he nudged one of the pears, gently bumping its stem so as not to bruise the fruit or break off the thin twiggy branch it hung from. On the third poke the pear suddenly dropped past his cheek and landed on the ground with a thud.

'Here,' he said. He picked up the pear and brought it over. 'Try that.'

I bit into it and he smiled in anticipation.

'Good, huh?'

'Delicious,' I said. It really was.

'What did I tell you?'

They both observed me as I ate the pear. Mrs Sforza had her head tilted back and leaned to one side, her bushy white eyebrows floating high up on her forehead as she enjoyed my pleasure, gazing at me with a fond look. I had to smile at the way she was looking, and when she saw me smile, her mouth spread into a grin.

I told them I had to think about going, that I had to catch a bus to New York to pick up some darkroom supplies for the assignment I had been given.

'You don't have to go yet,' Mr Sforza said.

'I'll be back. This isn't exactly my last visit,' I said. 'About that suicide – when was that?'

'Let's see, that must have been around the end of the sixties. I think it was 1968 or '69. You weren't even born yet. Sit down.'

'I was born in 1970.'

'Listen, sit down. Yeah, your brother Pete – may his soul rest in peace – was around in those days but you weren't born yet. Your mother and father were practically newlyweds. Pete was about three months old when your father tried to commit suicide.'

'The Pulaski Skyway,' I said. I tried to visualise the scene of my father leaning over the railing a couple of hundred feet above the river.

'Right over the Hackensack river – not the Passaic, the Hackensack. Take a look as you go by some time and you'll see where your father got stopped by the cops. Listen, stay put for a while. We're not finished here yet.'

'Jersey City cops,' Mrs Sforza said.

'Jersey City cops, Hoboken cops, Newark cops – cops are cops,' Mr Sforza said.

'Cops are cops, all right,' she said. 'Listen, we have cheesecake for dessert.' Mrs Sforza bounced her eyebrows up and down like Groucho: the smiling siren enticing me. 'From Hansen's. Made this morning. Still warm.'

'That's right. You can't go yet,' Mr Sforza said. 'We have this cheesecake we have to eat.'

'Well, Hansen's,' I said. 'Can't refuse that. But then I have to go, really.'

'Sure. We don't want to keep you,' Mr Sforza said, 'but you're welcome to stay as long as you like.'

Mrs Sforza served a thin creamy wedge so quiveringly tall on the serving spoon it was structurally unsound. As she handed the plate across the table, the wedge fluffed over on its side. Nobody made cheesecakes as deep and as light and as fluffy as Hansen's. She served her husband and herself smaller slices, laying theirs flat.

'We're pigging out,' she said. 'Retirement's living.'

She had worked for years as a seamstress in a Jersey City dress factory and, after seven years of retirement, still couldn't get over the luxury of doing nothing.

'Mm – really good,' Mr Sforza said, swallowing a mouthful. 'That Hansen's – really good stuff. With a cheesecake like this, it's all in the ingredients you use and the way you prepare them.'

'How is that different from the rest of cooking?' his wife asked.

He laughed. 'Ah, she's too smart for me. What are you going to New York for?'

'I need chemicals and paper. And film is cheaper when you buy a whole lot all at once.'

'It must be a fascinating field to be able to do photography. What is this, a wedding assignment?'

I said the phone call that had delayed me was about a freelance job for a series the *Journal* was doing on the changing suburbs.

'I gotta hand it to you Castellanos – all that talent. Our two boys, one's a building contractor and the other one runs a gas station.'

'Two gas stations now,' Mrs Sforza said.

'Listen,' I said, 'I wish *I* knew how to build a house. There's some repairs I need to have done.'

'No, I don't mean that. They're both honest and they're both good family men.'

'Well?' Mrs Sforza said. 'Isn't that what counts?'

'Sure, I'm not saying that – no complaints, except that one's in Ohio and one's in Indiana. And when you want to see your grandchildren… But they're fine boys. Here, take some more cheesecake.'

'Yeah, that's true,' Mrs Sforza said. 'One's in Ohio and one's in Indiana. You have to drive all the way across Pennsylvania to get to Ohio. Jesus.'

As Mrs Sforza served me another piece of cake, only just slightly smaller than the first, I watched a blue jay glide silently across the yard to a soft landing at the top of the pear tree. As the jay looked over at us the small branch it had landed on dipped and swayed under the impact.

'Beat it!' Mr Sforza yelled. He flailed his arms. The jay took off soundlessly. 'They're very loud birds,' he explained. 'Once they start jabbering and squawking… I know they're only communicating with each other, but still.'

'Yeah,' Mrs Sforza said. 'Noisy bastards.'

I said, 'Well, I really better be going. If I can move after this meal.'

'We don't want to keep you. We know you have to go. You sure you're OK health-wise? Eating properly?' Mr Sforza said.

'You're not keeping me – yes, I'm fine.'

'Because we're like parents to you. Remember that.'

'Campobass' people,' Mrs Sforza said to me, 'they have this thing about health. They have to keep asking you if you're healthy.'

Feeling full hadn't spoiled my pleasure in putting away the second piece but now I felt heavy. As I cleaned off the plate I saw, over Mr Sforza's shoulder, an old man appear in a backyard two houses down. He was with a little girl of about five or six, probably his granddaughter. She was leading him by the hand and exaggeratedly taking giant steps and chanting. It was obvious the grandfather was enjoying being with her. He trailed her loose-jointedly, playing the clown – or maybe he was pretending to be drunk. Maybe he was.

'Ya-ya,' he said to her.

'Ya-ya,' she mimicked back, laughing.

'Ya-ya.'

'Ya-ya,' she said joyfully.

'Ya-ya.'

'YA-YA,' she screamed happily, and began dragging him back inside, doing giant steps in a zigzag line as she pulled him. The yard was silent again.

'Ben Hanford,' Mrs Sforza said quietly, 'Ida's father. Haven't seen him in months.'

'Retired fifteen years now,' Mr Sforza said. 'Way back he used to work for the old Lehigh, I think, or the Lackawanna. Bad diabetes.'

'Why don't you go over and ask him how his health is?'

'He was named in some kind of bookkeeping scandal – I forget. But he's a good man. He was crazy about his wife, poor thing. And you can tell he really loves his daughter and granddaughter.'

I was crazy about my wife too, I was thinking. I tried not to think about her.

'I like that story about my father,' I said to Mr Sforza.

'I knew you would,' he said enthusiastically. 'Can you imagine those cops thinking he'd jump in the river?'

'Listen, not to be impolite,' Mrs Sforza said to her husband as she got up from the table, 'but before you take us all out to the Pulaski Skyway again, I have some house cleaning to do.'

'This is Sunday.'

'I forgot to do it yesterday, what can I tell you? See you, Michael,' she said. She waved goodbye and disappeared into the kitchen.

Mr Sforza and I had started to say goodbye when we heard a vacuum cleaner whining from an upstairs window.

'Don't mind her,' Mr Sforza said. 'Sunday. It's senility, I think. But it could be the new false teeth. They're killing her, you know.'

The vacuuming stopped abruptly. Mrs Sforza's head stuck out of a second-floor window. 'Michael,' she called down to me, 'I don't want you to think I'm rude leaving like that, OK?' She waved again.

'You weren't rude, Mrs Sforza,' I said, waving back.

She flashed her teeth and stood at the window looking down at us. I could see why he loved her – his OK wife.

'How are you these days?' I said to Mr Sforza.

'No point complaining. My father always used to say that people from Campobass' can take whatever happens in life. Like your father – well, he wasn't from Campobass' but he had a cousin there. Anyway, he almost went bankrupt once, back in the seventies, but he sprang back. You couldn't keep him down. Did he ever tell you about the Arizona land deal?'

'No.'

'Maybe next time I'll tell you about the Arizona land deal. Not even bankruptcy could stop your father.'

'It sounds like not even suicide could stop him,' I said.

Mr Sforza laughed at the joke and yelled up: 'Hey, Clara, did you hear that? Not even suicide could stop his father.'

Mrs Sforza looked at her husband, then looked at me and tapped her temple.

'Aaah,' her husband said. 'She gets that way. I tell everybody it's her false teeth but I'm beginning to think it's maybe her senility coming on.'

She heard that. 'At least I've got the false teeth. What's your excuse?'

'*Ciao*,' I said to them and left.

'*Ciao.*'

I first crossed over to my house to pick up my chequebook. A few minutes later, as I headed for the bus stop to catch the bus that would take me to the Port Authority, I could hear Mr Sforza clattering dishes and slamming pans into the sink as the vacuum cleaner whined away upstairs. Through the open kitchen door Mr Sforza saw me cut through the alley behind the houses.

'Don't forget next time,' he shouted, coming to the door. 'I'll tell you that story.'

'What?'

'I'll tell you the bankruptcy story,' he yelled.

The vacuuming stopped and Mrs Sforza's head appeared at the window.

'What?' she asked.

Mr Sforza stepped outside the door and looked up. 'Nothing. I said I love you.' He had a big smile.

Mrs Sforza flashed her teeth at him and saw me at the back

fence. She waved goodbye again and pointed at her husband and tapped her temple.

'Yeah, yeah, I know,' I heard Mr Sforza say. I could tell he was beaming. 'You love me too.'

'Ha!' she said and went on with her vacuuming.

Sunday comes and Sunday goes, I thought. The bus stop was only a block away and as I walked I could still hear the vacuuming – a pleasant sound.

contributors

Hiag Akmakjian is a photographer, a New Yorker, and author of a novel, *30,000 Mornings*, and a book of translations from the Japanese: *Snow Falling from a Bamboo Leaf: The Art of Haiku*. He lives in Wales.

Christopher Coake is the author of the story collection *We're in Trouble* (Harcourt, 2005). He lives in Reno with his wife and two dogs, and teaches creative writing at the University of Nevada.

Fictioneer and journalist **Katherine Dunn** is probably most familiar for her third novel, *Geek Love*.

Mary Gaitskill is the author of the novels *Two Girls, Fat and Thin* and *Veronica*, as well as the story collections *Bad Behavior* and *Because They Wanted To*. Her story 'Secretary' was the basis for the feature film of the same name.

Rebecca Godfrey is the author of the novel *The Torn Skirt* and the true crime book *Under the Bridge*. She lives in New York.

noise

Laird Hunt is the author of three novels, *The Impossibly*; *Indiana, Indiana* and *The Exquisite*.

Shelley Jackson is the author of *Half Life*, *The Melancholy of Anatomy*, hypertexts including the classic *Patchwork Girl*, two children's books, and *Skin*, a story published in tattoos on 2,095 volunteers, one word at a time. She is co-founder of the Interstitial Library and headmistress of the Shelley Jackson Vocational School for Ghost Speakers and Hearing-Mouth Children. She lives in Brooklyn and at www.ineradicablestain.com.

J. Robert Lennon is the author of six novels, including *Happyland*, serialised in 2006 in *Harper's* magazine and the forthcoming *Castle*. He lives in central New York State.

Samuel Ligon is the author of the novel *Safe in Heaven Dead* (HarperCollins), and the editor of *Willow Springs*. His stories have appeared in *Post Road*, *StoryQuarterly*, *Other Voices*, *Alaska Quarterly Review*, and elsewhere. He teaches at Eastern Washington University in Spokane.

Emily Maguire is the author of two novels: *Taming the Beast* and *The Gospel According to Luke*. Her essays on sex, religion and literature have appeared in the *Sydney Morning Herald* and the *Observer*.

Tom McCarthy is the author of two novels, *Remainder* and *Men in Space*, and a non-fiction book, *Tintin and the Secret of Literature*. He is also General Secretary of the International Necronautical Society (INS).

Scott Mebus is author of *The Big Happy* and *The Booty Nomad*, a musician, screenwriter, scorer and TV producer.

Eileen Myles' latest collection of poems, *Sorry, Tree,* will be out from wave books this spring. She's been living both in southern CA and NY since 2002, teaching at UCSD. Each week this year she'll be blogging on art at http://openfordesign.msn.com.

Catherine O'Flynn was born in Birmingham, England in 1970. She has variously been a child detective, a mystery customer, a victim of squirrels and a music enthusiast. Her first novel, *What Was Lost*, was published in 2007.

Lee Ranaldo is a visual artist, writer and member of Sonic Youth, who continues to record new music and tour the world on a regular basis. His visual art and sound works have been shown at galleries and museums around the world. His latest collection of poems is *Hello from The American Desert*, in which Internet spam is enlisted as a springboard for poetry. *Maelstrom from Drift*, a new solo CD, is forthcoming in summer 2008.

Emily Carter Roiphe is the award-winning author of *Glory Goes and Gets Some* available in the UK from Serpent's Tail. She is attempting another book and, in the meantime, enjoys her work as a freelance cultural critic (who doesn't?). She lives in Minneapolis with her life partner and two dogs, all three of them strays.

Kevin Sampsell lives in Portland, Oregon, and runs the micro-press Future Tense Books. His fiction and essays have appeared in a wide variety of journals and newspapers throughout the US. His books include *Beautiful Blemish* and *Creamy Bullets*.

Steven Sherrill paints, writes, parents, teaches and struggles with his banjo in Altoona, Pennsylvania.

Matt Thorne is the author of six novels: *Tourist* (1998), *Eight Minutes Idle* (1999, winner of an Encore Prize), *Dreaming of Strangers* (2000), *Pictures of You* (2001), *Child Star* (2003) and *Cherry* (2005, long-listed for the Booker Prize.) He also co-edited the anthologies *All Hail the New Puritans* (2000) and *Croatian Nights* (2005), and has written three books for children.

Rachel Trezise was born in South Wales in 1978. Her first novel, *In and Out of the Goldfish Bowl*, was an Orange Futures Prize winner. Her collection of short stories, *Fresh Apples*, won the EDS Dylan Thomas Prize. She is also author of the memoir/rockumentary *Dial M for Merthyr: On Tour with Midasuno*. She is currently working on her second novel.

Jess Walter's four novels include *The Zero*, which was a finalist for the 2006 National Book Award, and *Citizen Vince*, 2005 Edgar Award winner for best novel.

Peter Wild is the co-author of *Before the Rain* and the editor of *Perverted by Language: Fiction inspired by The Fall* and *The Flash*. Read more at www.peterwild.com.

acknowledgements

The editor would like to thank Sonic Youth, Pete Ayrton, John Williams, Rebecca Gray, Matt Thorne, Niamh Murray, Ruthie Petrie, Richard Thomas, David Gaffney, Sarah Hymas, Emily Carter Roiphe, Moshe Levy, Tom McCarthy, Tony O'Neill, Ben Myers, Nathan Tyree, Arthur Nersesian, Carlton Mellick III, Mitch Cullin, Paul Di Fillippo, Ewan Morrison, Catherine O'Flynn, Pru Rowlandson, Gary Ramsay and (as ever) Louisa, Harriet, Samuel & Martha.